MW01610889

PROTECTING MARI (SPECIAL FORCES: OPERATION ALPHA)

CARA CARNES

Cover Design by Freya Barker at RE&D
Editing by Heather Long & Ink It Out Editing

Dear Readers,

Welcome to the Special Forces: Operation Alpha Fan-Fiction world!

If you are new to this amazing world, in a nutshell the author wrote a story using one or more of my characters in it. Sometimes that character has a major role in the story, and other times they are only mentioned briefly. This is perfectly legal and allowable because they are going through Aces Press to publish the story.

This book is entirely the work of the author who wrote it. While I might have assisted with brainstorming and other ideas about which of my characters to use, I didn't have any part in the process or writing or editing the story.

I'm proud and excited that so many authors loved my characters enough that they wanted to write them into their own story. Thank you for supporting them, and me!

READ ON!
    Xoxo
    Susan Stoker

CHAPTER 1

RED AND BLUE SIRENS SPUN AROUND HER, MARRING the otherwise serene early morning in Austin, Texas. Marisol Santos yanked on the frayed edges of the hastily donned t-shirt and willed an end to the nightmare as she studied the dance of blue and red along the cracked pavement outside Shady Apartments.

The colors should inspire security and comfort, but they didn't. Not for Mari.

Another vehicle arrived, an unmarked one. Dread clawed her insides, wrapped around her lungs, and squeezed until every breath was pained.

No, that wasn't dread. It was a war wound—one of many she'd collected when hell broke loose. Her gaze swept to the long, windy route leading to the front of the complex. The lone path back to her patch of existence remained empty. "There's fingerprints. I can show you where."

"Ma'am, I'm afraid we can't call out a crime unit. Procedure is very clear. Without blood or fluids on scene, there's nothing we can do, especially not for a theft." The beat cop's lips thinned as he scrawled something else in his pad. "Are you sure there's no one I can call for you?"

She swallowed and somehow forced her mind past what he'd just said. There'd be no crime scene unit because the only crime tonight per his little notebook was the loss of a cell phone. Loyalty ran deep in brothers in blue, a fact she'd learned long, long ago, but that didn't stop her from trying one more time. "There's fingerprints. I can show you where."

The man's lips thinned once more. "Very well, show me."

Another layer of numb settled around her, shielding her from his placating tone. Mari followed his progression into her open apartment door. "Someone keeps leaving the door open. My cat."

That someone was likely the cop's partner who'd spent more time tromping in and out of her place than anyone. To say the Austin Police Department was less than interested someone had broken into her tiny unit at 3:04 a.m. was an understatement. The fact the bastard had...

Nope. Not going there.

So she focused on the danged door. In terms of obsession, it'd become her primary one. Worrying about June Bug fleeing the small one-bedroom like any sane-minded person or animal would kept her mind off the real troubles—troubles the young cop in front of her wasn't picking up on even though she'd tried every which way to get the discussion moving.

Without blood or fluids on scene, there's nothing we can do, especially not for a theft.

She repeated his words in her mind, accepted them as a brick wall, one she'd slammed up against enough to know it wouldn't crumble easily. She'd officially reached the end of her rope, though. Admitting defeat wasn't something she did. Where there was a will, there was a way.

She studiously pointed to where she knew the bastard had touched. The officer nodded, but his lack of desire to do anything about the potential fingerprints spiked her anger. She was so far in over her head she'd likely drowned months ago and simply hadn't noticed.

"Can I borrow a phone? I need to make a call." She held her hand out expectantly.

The young beat cop had no idea who she was, who her ex was. To him she was merely another incident report he'd have to fill out before he got to go home and crawl into bed.

But an unmarked police car had just arrived, which meant someone entrenched deeper within blue had arrived on scene. Her anonymity was about to expire, which meant she only had a few moments to phone for help. Who would wade into this mess she called a life and keep her safe from a crazy stalking ex-husband high up within the Austin Police Department?

The cell phone settled into her outstretched palm, and for the first time since the incident occurred, she felt something aside from shock, fear and anger.

Hope.

She only knew one badass with the ability to take on the APD. The only problem was he was stationed overseas with his unit. Or team. She wasn't sure what they called themselves, and she didn't much care. Joseph was the best big brother she could ask for, which was why she'd had to be smart and not let him know how bad things had gotten between her and her ex-husband, Chester.

Mari moved away from the officer to get a bit of privacy, not that it mattered. She didn't care if he heard the conversation because it was a last-ditch effort to get help. The number was one she'd memorized a few weeks ago when her brother had offered it up. A contact. A man Joe knew, one who knew lots and lots of people.

It was terribly early in the morning, and she wasn't sure where the phantom named Tex lived, but he was literally her only hope at this point. Fear clawed her insides as her gaze swept the parking lot. Dread settled like a lead balloon as she locked gazes with Paul Gomez, Chester's former partner.

"Hello." The voice on the other end was deep and alert, despite the wretched hour.

"Erm, hi. I'm so, so sorry I know it's late. Or early, really. M-My brother gave me this number, said to call if I ever needed help." She stammered the words out as a tremble knocked her insides around and radiated outward until her entire body quaked. "I need Tex."

"You've got me. You're shaking so bad I can hear your teeth rattling through the phone. Take a deep breath for me."

"Afraid deep breaths aren't an option. I've got a couple cracked ribs." Her pulse steadied as silence settled on the other side of the phone. "Sorry, I'm screwing this up. I...my brother gave me this number. Joseph Santos, but you likely know him as Hazard."

"You're the sister, Marisol. He mentioned you'd been having some troubles with an ex."

"Yeah." She tightened. "I need help, but I'm not sure who to trust."

"There a reason you aren't phoning the cops about this?"

"He is one," she answered as her gaze settled on Paul Martin. *Crap.* "A sergeant in Homicide. I need help. Please."

She'd pull what little she had in savings. Somehow she'd come up with the money to get someone to help her. She squeezed the phone tighter and tracked Paul's progression as he made his way toward her.

She'd once really liked Paul, back when she'd still been with Chester and they'd been detectives in the Robbery Division. But he'd taken Chester's side, as expected, when the tumultuous divorce played out. Ever since then everyone in a uniform was persona non grata as far as she was concerned.

"You're at Shady Apartments in South Austin?" Tex asked.

"Yes." She didn't question how he knew. Joseph said Tex had wicked mojo, and her big brother had never steered her wrong before.

"I'm sending someone to you now. He's former military, he and his brother were both Deltas, the kind of men your brother would trust with his life. Or his little sister's."

Mari took a deeper breath and expended some of the stress. Someone was coming. She wasn't alone against an army of blue. "Thank you."

"They've got a good program, one meant to help people with their back against a wall and no way out of their mess. They knock down walls, Marisol."

"Mari." She took another breath. "My friends call me Mari."

"Well then, I'm honored to call you Mari. Your brother's team is in the middle of a mission right now. You want, I'll get word to him, see what I can do to get him stateside."

He could do that? Mari gulped, shook her head fiercely, then realized he couldn't see her. "No, don't. He can't do anything."

"I'm thinking Hazard would come up with quite a few things he could do," Tex clipped. "But Ethan and his brother Milo will likely do them all for him."

"Ethan and Milo?" Those didn't seem like kickass military names, where monikers like Hazard were more commonplace.

"Gemini. They'll get you sorted."

"Thank you."

"Call me once you're settled. On second thought, I'll have Gemini call me. He's en route, so ten minutes at most. Is that your cell you're calling from?" Silence, then he returned. "It's not. Where's yours?"

"The guy took it." She squeezed her eyes shut.

"Number?"

She rattled it off. "I can get another."

"That's good to know, and I'm sure Gemini will see that you do, but I'm working on finding the bastard who hurt you. You want, I'll hang on the line until he gets there."

"No. I-I'd better go." Paul came to a stop a couple steps away from her. "Thanks again."

She clicked off and handed the phone back to the beat cop when he returned. The young officer nodded his head and greeted Paul with a handshake.

"What've we got?" Paul asked.

"Intruder woke her. There was a struggle. He took off with her cellphone."

Another bolt of anger surged within her adrenaline-charged body. She fisted her hands and forced silence with a bite to her tongue. Paul didn't give a shit what had really happened. His disdain was a fourth presence within their cluster, so strong and palpable it was a punch to her resolve.

"Ms. Santos," Paul quipped. "It seems your decisions are catching up to you. This isn't the safest neighborhood for a recently single woman."

"You know Ms. Santos?" The beat cop's gaze narrowed.

"She divorced my former partner, Sergeant Rollins in Homicide." Hand on hip, he glanced around. "Pretty desolate back here. We have any witnesses?"

"No, sir."

"Very well." He reached into his pocket and pulled out a card. "Call me later today, Ms. Santos. We'll sit you down with a sketch artist."

"This isn't your division's investigation," she replied, her voice mottled with the anger she didn't bother hiding. How dare he come onto the scene and dismiss what'd happened. "You're Robbery."

"I think I know my job," Paul replied, a bite in his voice.

"He hit me and ripped my shirt off, then proceeded to force himself on me. That accelerates it out of the Robbery Division and into the Sex Crimes Unit, a fact I would have pointed out if the officer here had allowed me to give him more facts about what happened."

Paul's face reddened. "You were assaulted?"

She forced a nod. The beat cop shifted restlessly beside her.

"Sorry, Detective, she hadn't mentioned that."

"Ms. Santos has a history of falsifying facts." Paul's focus slid past Mari and to a presence behind her—one who'd just halted within the fringes of her peripheral vision. "This is a police investigation, sir. Head back into your apartment or leave. Your choice, but you can't be here."

"I'm not going anywhere until you're done with Ms. Santos, Detective."

The gravely voice startled Mari a moment because of its proximity. A hand settled on her shoulder. She looked up. And up. Geez, the man was tall, at least a foot taller than her height, which wasn't saying much since she was five two. A black t-shirt stretched across an incredibly wide chest. Muscles rippled along his arms.

His strong jawline flexed slightly as his gaze remained locked on Paul. She swallowed beneath the intensity etched on his handsome face. Protectiveness. It radiated from him in every action he took, the protective stance along her back, the slight touch of his hand at her shoulder.

She was no longer alone, and even though he was a stranger woken in the dead of the morning, he wanted her to know that fact. More importantly, he wanted *Paul* to know.

Her eyes burned as the tenuous grip she'd held on her emotions slipped a little beneath the stranger's rocksteady presence.

"I must've misunderstood you, Detective. I could swear I just heard you dismiss a victim's statement without investigating the facts. Fortunately for Ms. Santos, you won't be the investigator handling her cases. Ms. Santos and I will be over there until the proper division is called." His statement brooked no discussion. A firm hand touched her hip.

"I didn't catch a name," Paul said.

"Ethan Davenport," he replied. "I'm here on behalf of Counterstrike. Ms. Santos is in our protection now."

"Is that right?" Paul's mouth kicked up in a smug grin. "I hate to break it to you, Mr. Davenport, but Ms. Santos here exaggerates the truth. I'm aware of your group. You've done a lot for this community, and for the victims of domestic violence. She's not one of them."

"Is that so?"

Mari tensed beneath Paul's indignant and accusatory tone. Didn't military men and former soldiers hang tight with cops? Chester had known lots of former Army people, or so he claimed. She'd rarely seen any hang around with him at the house.

"If you'll come with me, Ms. Santos, I'll continue to take your statement." The beat cop glanced at Paul. "Sorry for the confusion, Detective."

Mari nodded and mutely followed behind the uniformed officer. Ethan, aka Gemini, remained at her side, hand on her back. For the first time since she'd woken up at 3:04 a.m. and touched an intruder's ear, she breathed deep.

Then winced as pain lanced her side.

But it didn't matter. She'd handle a little pain if it brought her closer to sealing the door shut on her nightmare.

❄

ETHAN PROWLED THE AREA OUTSIDE THE SECOND curtained examination room at South Austin's emergency room. Though the waiting room had been packed, he'd managed to get Marisol expedited thanks to Daphne, a woman Counterstrike had helped a few months ago. It was one of the main reasons he'd chosen the hospital over its counterpart closer to his home.

He pulled out his cell and punched the first name under his favorites. As always, Milo answered on the first ring. Big brother by two minutes never messed around with waiting for the second ring, especially not when they had a client in need of their help. "The safehouses on Manor and Shady Lane are both available and ready for use."

"She's coming home with me. None of the safehouses have security."

"Neither does our place," Milo replied.

"We'll be there. That'll do until we can get a bead on systems."

"Guess this favor for Tex is a bit more involved than we realized."

That was an understatement. "Her ex is a cop from what I gathered. We need to get more from Tex."

"We've got data coming in." Milo paused. 'He's a

sergeant in Homicide. Divorce was messy, restraining orders."

"Kids?"

"No," Milo responded. "Her status?"

"A battered face and a couple of broken ribs." He paused his pacing and growled the rest into the phone. "Bite marks on her breasts and chest area. Potential hairline fracture of her forearm. She was taken to x-ray to confirm the arm and ribs."

"Did they call in a crime scene unit?"

"Yes, grudgingly. They collected her clothing and are processing the apartment for prints." Ethan stared down the hall where they'd taken Mari.

He should have insisted on remaining with her. She'd slipped in and out of her head since his arrival. One minute she was alert and standing her ground with the cops and the next she was zoned.

Shock.

"Will she be okay at our place with just the two of us, or should I call Jen and have her get a guestroom at her place next door ready?"

Their little sister, Jen, lived next door in a small three-bedroom bungalow. They'd acquired both properties and spent a small fortune overhauling them. Given their location within highly sought-after Hyde Park, it had been a great investment.

He and Milo had gone into business with Jen to form Counterstrike after they'd left the service a year before. Though they were still getting situated, they'd managed to solidify themselves within the Austin metroplex as the best nonprofit resource for victims of domestic violence, and anyone else needing help in situations where they were the underdog. No one should suffer because they couldn't afford help.

"We'll likely need her help at some point, but don't wake her until I assess the situation closer. So far Marisol's not exhibiting signals she's nervous around me. I think we'll be fine. Get the guest room on my floor ready, though."

"Will do. I'll send a couple guys over to the apartment after the cops are finished. We can get Jessica to run prints and evidence we gather, as a secondary precaution."

Jessica Randolph was a family friend who'd started a private crime lab a few years earlier after her sister's murder investigation was botched because of faulty evidence handling. She left her cushy job in California as Assistant Chief Medical Examiner and founded Second Trace with a couple of her associates.

She offered pro bono work to them as her time

permitted, which was often since she was a workaholic dedicated to helping people uncover the truth she was denied.

Movement in Ethan's periphery drew his attention. He tracked Marisol's progression down the hall and toward him. Shoulders drawn inward, eyes cast downward, she trudged alongside the nurse, who seemed more impatient than situationally aware.

The woman in pink scrubs spoke fast and loud, but Ethan doubted Mari had heard a single word. She stopped when the nurse put a hand on her arm. Blinked.

"Do you have any questions?"

Mari shook her head.

"I'm going to need you to go over everything again with me," Ethan ordered. "In case you haven't noticed, she's in shock. She won't remember much of what you said."

"And you are?" The older woman peered at him over her glasses.

"A friend," he replied.

"Do you know him, ma'am?" The woman looked at Mari, who shuffled toward Ethan the moment he outstretched his arm.

She curled into his side and settled her head on his chest. Protectiveness swelled within him. He didn't know why she trusted him enough to do it, and he didn't much care. He'd fight the entire APD to keep her safe if that's what was needed.

The nurse sighed and went through the discharge paperwork a second time. Prescriptions in hand, Ethan made quick work of getting Mari out of the hospital and situated in his truck. The sooner he got her home where she could rest, the better. Sleep might prove difficult for her, but it would help her bruised body begin the healing process.

CHAPTER 2

A THUD WOKE HER.

June Bug was up to her troubles again. "Not now, June Bug, Momma needs her rest."

Mari reached out to stroke June Bug's soft fur. Her fingertips brushed across warmth. Hot, smooth skin. Weird. She stroked down, traced the distinctive curve.

Fear ignited her pulse as she yanked her hand back.

An ear.

She screamed.

Mari woke with a start. She pivoted out of the bed and crashed onto the floor. Pain rolled through her in angry, stab-like sensations along her side. Her heart thudded in her chest. Her pulse thrummed in her ears as her gaze flitted around the room.

Not her room.

"The lamp beside you is touch activated." The voice made her jump as she angled to her knees and peered toward the light spilling in from the doorway. A large shadow stood there, but the voice continued, stilling her thoughts. "You're safe, Marisol. I'm Ethan, we met at your place a few hours ago."

A few hours ago.

Right.

He'd taken on Paul and then insisted she go to the hospital.

Everything after that fuzzed in her brain. How had she gotten here? Where the heck was here?

"You fell asleep in my truck. You're at my house, in a guest room. You're safe, Marisol."

He repeated the latter once again, as if book ending the fact he'd started with. She focused on it, repeated it in a loop as she stood and looked down at the scrubs she barely remembered changing into after they'd taken pictures.

Pictures of the bite marks. The bruising—what little there was so far. The nurse said it'd take a while for the worst of them to show. She'd given Mari a number of where to text pictures of them when they did.

She'd have to send pictures of her naked, bitten to hell, bruised breasts to a stranger's number. She swallowed and forced her mind away from those particular thoughts.

"I'm sorry I fell asleep," she whispered, unsure exactly how that had happened. She'd thought she'd never sleep again, yet she'd literally gone so comatose she'd fallen asleep in a stranger's truck.

He'd freaking carried her into his house, or she assumed as much since she had no clue how she would've gotten inside otherwise.

Adrenaline surged within her as her fight or flight response kicked in again. The damn thing activated instantaneously. Slow reactions resulted in pain, and she'd never been a big fan of that.

Chester wouldn't be too happy that she'd filed a police report. He'd send someone else to hurt her. That someone would hurt anyone between her and him. The thought spiraled her mind onto a new path.

Ethan had been nice, he'd gotten her away when she needed to go anywhere but where she was at. But she couldn't let him or anyone else get hurt by Chester and the assholes who did his bidding.

"I should go." She yanked on the bottom of her scrubs even though everything was hanging where it should. The sooner she got away from Ethan, the better for him. "Thanks for your help."

He angled away from the entry, as if offering her room to pass. Arms crossed, his full lips thinned into a grim line. "You're not leaving, Marisol."

"Mari," she corrected. "Friends call me Mari, and anyone who stands up against my ex's asshole friends gets to be mine, whether they want to or not."

"Well, Mari, I was raised to believe friends didn't abandon friends having troubles. And you, sweetheart, have a big pile of those slithering all around you like an angry nest of vipers." He took a couple steps into the room, toward the curtains and pulled them open. Sunlight filtered in from the outside, bathing the area in warm, refreshing rays. "There's a bathroom behind you. My sister Jen lives next door. She brought over some clothes for you to use, but the pants might be a bit long. She's taller than you."

Mari glanced over at the pile of clothes on the edge of a gorgeous cherry wood dresser. Shock coiled through her as June Bug crawled from underneath the bed and wound around her feet. She fell to her knees and hugged her kitty close as moisture burned within her watery gaze.

"I asked Twitch to bring her here, figured she'd be happier with you," the man commented. "And seeing a friendly face when you're waking up somewhere strange is always welcome, especially after you've had a scare."

She looked around the immaculate room, then down at her long-haired menace. To say June Bug was a troublemaker was an understatement. "Thank you. I'll make sure she behaves. I can keep her locked in her carrier."

"There's no need. She's already explored the whole house while you've been asleep. She and Chompers have reached a tentative understanding."

"Chompers?"

Ethan whistled, low and long. The click clack of nails across hardwood floors echoed from down the hall. She drew June Bug closer and stood as a massive German Shepherd entered the small bedroom. Tongue lolling to the side, Chompers sat on his ass at Ethan's feet and stared at Mari and June Bug.

She rubbed June Bug's head and took a step closer to the gorgeous dog watching her with such curiosity and enthusiasm, his entire body trembled. He whined low but remained in position. Ethan made a gesture and the animal rose, taking a step to close the distance.

And sniffed her outstretched hand. A few ear scratches later and she and Chompers were the best of buds. June Bug, on the other hand, wasn't a fan. She hissed and growled her mock anger.

"Don't mind her, she's always growly at first, then she adapts," Mari commented. "I foster dogs and kitties waiting for permanent homes quite a bit." She bit her lip as regret filled her. "Or I used to."

"We'll get you back to the life you deserve to have and away from the one you've been forced into, Mari. It might take some effort, and fuck knows it won't be pleasant for you, not by any stretch of the imagination." Ethan took a couple steps forward, reached out and ran a hand along the side of her face.

The tentative graze of his fingertips sent a shockwave of awareness rippling through her. The gentle glide along the undamaged portion of her face made her heart thud hard in her chest. June Bug began purring in her arms.

"Whoever did this," he whispered, "will pay tenfold. No one strikes a woman and gets by with it."

God.

The fierceness and ironclad confidence he exuded tumbled from him in thick, comforting waves. He had no doubt he'd find the bastard who'd hurt her. For the first time since she'd been woken at

3:04 a.m., she had a firm grip on hope. Determination. Resolve.

It would be okay because her brother's friend Tex had made it so by calling Ethan Davenport, aka Gemini. She swallowed the thank you lodged in her throat. She'd already expressed her gratitude and knew that if the man before her was anything like her brother, he wouldn't want to hear it too often.

You don't thank a man like me for doing my job, sis.

She'd find a better way to express her gratitude somehow. For now, she'd graciously accept the help he offered, whatever that might be.

"I'll be downstairs in the kitchen. You okay with omelets for a late brunch?"

Her stomach rumbled. Heat rose in her face as he flashed a sexy grin that singed her clear to her toes. Damn. Ethan Davenport was dangerous to the senses, the kind of temptation she'd been sorely lacking in her life for months.

No, years.

Awareness beaded in tiny goosebumps along her arms as he took June Bug from her, like he'd been a lifelong friend to the finicky feline and not a total stranger. Any apprehension she'd had about Ethan died when the cat rubbed her head against the man's hand.

June Bug had always hated Chester. She'd been a kitten back then, one she'd saved from a watery grave. It'd been by a twist of bad luck she'd met Chester, who'd been doing a brief stint in the Animal Cruelty unit of APD to help cover a shortage. Going out for coffee with him had been the first big mistake of her life.

Marrying him had been the biggest mistake of the century.

She pushed back the unwanted memories and padded into the bathroom. The sooner she showered and changed, the sooner she could figure out what the hell to do. Someone had broken into her home.

Hurt her.

At least you weren't raped.

The nurse's comment from earlier echoed in her brain. Yeah, she hadn't been raped by the bastard. She stripped off her clothes and stepped into the massive shower. Warmth seeped into her as the water sprayed downward in a soft, slow patter resembling rain. She reached up and adjusted the showerhead until it became a torrential downpour that more matched the emotional upheaval rising in her throat.

Arms curled to her bite-riddled chest, she cried.

Alone in a stranger's shower, she sobbed and silently thanked whatever divine fate had finally given her a semblance of assistance in the form of a stranger named Tex.

And Ethan Davenport.

She hadn't divulged everything to the officer who took her statement earlier. She hadn't been ready, and she'd doubted he would have bothered to write it down.

But she needed to give the truth to someone. She wasn't just guessing that the bastard who'd broken in was sent by her ex. She knew. The bastard who'd hurt her made sure she knew who to thank for his arrival in her nightmares.

Chester says hello, cunt.

She'd locked away that portion of the hell deep, tucking it away so she'd survive the ordeal with the APD. No one there would give a damn or believe her, not when their golden boy Chester was involved.

Sooner or later she'd have to share the truth with someone or move the hell on. She couldn't give her asshole ex-husband the satisfaction of winning this battle, not when he'd won almost every other one so far. She may have divorced him, but he was never, ever going to leave her be.

"You want me to go in there?" Jen asked quietly as she came to a halt where Ethan stood just outside the hall.

He'd returned to make sure Mari found the towels, but the sounds of her violent sobs filtered into the hallway. He shook his head. The woman needed help, but for now, she needed time alone to come to terms with the fact the war she waged was no longer solely hers.

"I need to make a call." He pulled out his cell and headed downstairs before he lost all semblance of control and went into the bathroom. The urge to draw the beautiful woman into his arms and hold her was damn near impossible to ignore.

"I've got a friend digging into Chester," Tex said the moment he picked up. "Say the word and my buddy in the Texas Rangers will be all over this asshole."

Although Ethan would love nothing more than to sic the Texas Rangers on Mari's ex-husband, he wanted to play this smart in a way that would give the woman a permanent exit from the bastard. "We need a firmer grasp on what this assault was. I want that bastard first, then we'll deal with the asshole ex."

"The two are likely connected. Either that or she's the unluckiest woman in Austin," Tex commented. "Three cars vandalized, two totaled from the damage. Two break-ins at two other apartments—all in the span of a year and a half since the divorce finalized. The bastard kept her in court long enough to chew through her savings. Credit cards are maxed. She's working two jobs, neither pay anything close to what she needs to tread water."

"How much?"

"I'm not giving you this so you can wash it away courtesy of Davenport dollars," Tex replied.

"I'm not sitting back and letting her drown when I can clear the debt with a day's worth of interest off money I couldn't care less about." He glanced at his brother, who froze mid-chop. "How much?"

Eyebrows raised, Milo made no qualms about the fact he was listening in. Ethan pushed the speaker button so Tex's voice boomed within the area. The money wasn't just Ethan's, which meant he owed Milo a chance to weigh in.

"You do this, it can't be undone."

"Break it down for us," Ethan requested.

"Legal fees alone are well into five figures, but

there's a mountain of credit card debt. Beth's pulling the details. Some scumbag fly-by-night lawyer has her bent over with a twenty percent interest rate from what we've dug up," Tex said. "All together, we're looking at close to sixty. She's done a hell of a job trying to keep her head above water, but she's drowning. And from what I can see, her bastard ex is holding her head under to make sure she does it quick."

Ethan's gaze flicked to Milo, whose jaw twitched. Lips thinned, he offered a brief nod, then went back to chopping with more force than necessary.

"Wash it away, whatever it takes. You've got access to what you need."

He, Milo and Jen had agreed Counterstrike was the best way to use the old man's blood money. Mari's situation involved an abusive cop, though, which meant things had ramped up to an entirely new level of potential problems, one they'd needed to address long ago.

The security systems they used were total shit.

"We've avoided an overhaul of our security systems long enough, Tex. I need to know who's the best. No expense spared."

"It's about time. Dinosaurs had better systems than that shit your mom's buddy installed."

Ethan couldn't argue.

"You've got a few options, all top of the line," Tex commented. "I hoped you'd want to take this plunge, so I looked into an option too good to pass up a couple weeks ago."

The man's voice was hesitant, an uncommon occurrence. "And that is? Spit it out."

"The Mason brothers are running a new operation, three hours south of you, in Resino where they grew up. They're solid in a way no one can deny."

Fuck.

Ethan squeezed his eyes shut and willed the memories away. Nolan Mason.

He hadn't heard the name since he'd gotten dragged out of the jungle half dead. No, he hadn't been dragged out. He'd been carried out by Nolan Mason.

The man's team had been stranded, left for dead after the mission went sideways. He'd never gotten details because by the time he'd woken up in a hospital they were gone.

"You good?" Texas asked.

"Yeah," Ethan lied as his gaze slid to his brother, who wasn't chopping anymore.

Big brother by two minutes didn't appreciate the fact Ethan hadn't shared much about what went down in that jungle. He'd gotten back to a new team and been back in the thick of service as fast as possible—anything to forget the fact his entire team had been killed and he'd been the sole survivor.

The team he'd trained with.

But the new assignment had landed him on Milo's team and Gemini had been born. To say they'd taken shit from their teammates was an understatement, but Ethan had to admit he wouldn't have changed much of it if given another chance.

Except for the events that led Nolan's team into that jungle to drag his half-dead ass back to safety. He owed the man a bigger debt than he could ever repay.

And was apparently about to add to it.

"They're solid."

Tex's firm statement was all Ethan needed to hear, not that there'd been any doubt in his mind. If Nolan's brothers were anything like him, they were more than solid. "Make the call."

"It's more complicated than that. Their system isn't for sale. The back office operatives who designed it are the best in the business, a one hundred percent success rate. Every country including ours wants that system."

"And you mention this shit because..."

"Because the girl I know there thinks she can get you a tamed down version of it," Tex said. "She can't make any promises, but she's looking into it."

"And plan B?"

"I'll get to work on it, but it won't be anywhere near as good as plan A."

"Understood." Ethan clicked off and shoved his phone in his pocket.

"You look like you just chatted with a ghost."

"Close to it," he admitted.

"Mason." Milo started chopping a red bell pepper. "Is that the same Mason from your rescue?"

"Yeah." Ethan didn't offer more and was grateful when Milo took the hint. Now wasn't the time to dig up the past. "I'll be back, gonna go for a jog."

"You sure you wanna leave Marisol here with me? We haven't met."

"You'll manage." Ethan fisted his hands. "I need to burn off some of the ugly in my brain."

"Go. I'll cover for you."

Back before the service they'd been interchangeable. No one could tell them apart. They dressed alike, talked the same, even listened to the same music and had the same friends. Two halves of the same whole.

In many respects nothing had changed.

In others...well, neither of them was the man they'd once been. Now their similarities were more skin-deep than to the bone like they'd once been. The sooner he ran off the ugly, the sooner he could get back to Mari.

CHAPTER 3

MARI STOOD AT THE ENTRY TO THE KITCHEN AND watched the man chopping. He looked like a badass chef, a clone of Ethan.

But he wasn't Ethan. The subtle differences drew her attention: the extra stubble along his jawline, the tattoo along his arm. It was the same dragon, but with green instead of red.

He wasn't Ethan.

Chompers didn't seem to give a damn. He padded into the kitchen and drew the man's attention. She swallowed and took another step closer. He paused the rhythmic move of his knife, flashing a grin. "Hi there."

"Hi. I'm Mari." She forced a smile, even though it hurt. "I'm assuming you're a brother of Ethan's?"

The grin deepened, accentuating the handsomeness of his face. "That obvious?"

The tease made her laugh, which hurt even more. God, he and Ethan were so, so similar. But this man's eyes weren't haunted like Ethan's had been. He exuded confidence, but in a lighter, more relaxed way than Ethan had.

"You can tell us apart. That's a first. Even Mom has trouble some days." He smirked as if finding immense pleasure and amusement from the feat she'd accomplished. "I'm Milo, Ethan's elder by two minutes, aka the better half of Gemini."

Gemini. Of course. Now the moniker made sense.

"It's the eyes," she admitted as she looked around, trying to disguise the fact she really wanted to know where the man's twin had gone. "And the dragon. Yours is greener."

Had they both been in the military together? Questions rolled into perfect formation and started a queue within her mind.

"You've got a good eye for detail," he commented. "Jen's next door. I can grab her if you want."

"Jen?"

"Our little sister. She's an attorney who helped us start up Counterstrike."

"Counterstrike?"

Milo paused and studied her face a moment. "You have no clue what I'm talking about."

"No, sorry."

"Don't be. Sit." He motioned to a barstool near him. She hauled her short, plumper than she wanted self onto it and forced a polite smile as she eyed the door behind him and remembered the one to her back. He followed her line of sight and raised his eyebrows.

"My bedside manner's never been good, but women don't often want to flee my company, sweetheart. You're safe here. No one's going to hurt you, most especially me. Ethan would kick my ass."

"Good to know."

"How do you know Tex?" Milo asked.

"He's a friend of my brother I guess."

"Your brother's in the service."

"Yeah, but I can't give you details. He's never been able to tell me much about what he does."

"He knows Tex. That tells me all I need to know," Milo commented. "He wouldn't have called us if your brother wasn't tight with him."

"Thanks again for the help. I'll get out of your hair as soon as I can," she promised.

"Good luck with that," he commented with a

grin. "Little brother's burrowing into your mess much like Chompers when he has a new bone." Milo tossed the dog a piece of ham. "Ethan and I got out of the service about the same time. Little sis was pretty fed up with her corporate attorney world, so we decided to do something we wanted to do. Counterstrike was formed a few months later."

"What do you do at Counterstrike?"

"We help people in impossible situations, by any and all means necessary."

Wow. The fierceness in his statement calmed her, made her think of Joseph, who exuded the same lethal determination and quiet confidence.

"It must be nice to work with family," she commented.

"You tight with yours?"

"Yeah, Joseph's in the service. Mom and Dad are down in Florida testing out an early retirement. It's always been just the four of us."

"If you want to call them, we can make that happen. Jen's going to be bringing you a new cell phone when she comes over. Until then, make yourself at home. Make whatever calls you need to."

Work. Mari groaned. She'd done a no call, no show. Her boss would be beyond pissed, but it wasn't like anyone would miss her. With the university not in session, the UT libraries were pretty empty, except for the diligent graduate students working on their doctoral dissertations, or whatever all the brainiacs using the library did.

As far as work was concerned, it was quiet and peaceful—exactly the sort of thing she needed way more of in her life. Her second job at the coffee shop near the university was another story. Even though she worked the late-night shift, it was always a zoo—one she couldn't afford to miss, not even for a night. The tips were too good, and her boss there wasn't nearly as understanding.

"We help domestic violence victims mostly, especially those with children. Anyone with kids gets priority." Milo glanced at her. "Lots of people start making excuses for their exes right about now, when they're feeling safe and their mind starts playing tricks on them. They start thinking things like, 'Maybe it's not as bad as it seemed.'"

"It was." He froze, so she continued. "As bad as it seemed. Way, way worse."

The door behind Milo opened and a beautiful, long-legged brunette entered. Since Mari had rolled up the stretchy pants she'd donned at least four times and tested the boundaries of shoving her wide hips into the snug, but soft fabric, she suspected this was the woman who'd kindly lent her some clothes.

And the familial resemblance was evident. She had the same thick, gorgeous wavy hair as Ethan and Milo. Hers tumbled in soft curls Mari envied. Mari's always kinked way too much and frizzed in humidity. Curly hair sucked.

The woman stopped near her brother and her wide, expressive gaze was a bright green rather than the soft cinnamon, warmed chocolatey mix of Ethan's and Milo's. She wore a beautiful shade of pink lipstick so pale you could barely notice it if it weren't for her pale, creamy skin that shimmered like ivory.

"You must be Marisol."

"Mari."

"Right." The woman set her bag down and held out her hand. "I'm Jennifer, but everyone calls me Jen. I'm your new attorney."

Mari blinked.

"Mari missed a few things about what we do. I was going to wait until Ethan got back from his run to start filling in the blanks."

The woman's brow crinkled. "He went for a run?"

"Yeah, after chatting with Tex."

"What happened?" the woman asked.

39

"Leave it be, sis," Milo warned. "He won't leave us alone with Mari for long. We know all his secrets."

"Not all of them." Jen's concern rippled through the room and Mari couldn't help but tighten.

She recognized familial worry when she heard it, especially since she'd had loads of experience in the form of her parents and a big brother since she finally decided to leave Chester. She'd tossed her small family into the emotional wringer and taken them for more than their fair share of spins. Thank God they'd held on fiercely and never given up.

Ethan entered from the same doorway Jen had not too long ago. Sweat dampened his t-shirt and face. He grinned and held out his arms as he closed the distance between himself and Jen.

"Don't do it," the woman warned. "So help me God, I'll get you back, Ethan. Don't think I won't."

He chuckled and lunged. She squealed and kicked her legs as he drew her against his massive body and lifted her off the ground. Their laughter echoed within the kitchen. Milo chuckled as he continued adding stuff to two skillets on the stove.

Mari couldn't help but smile even though she felt as if she were invading their private sanctuary.

The two siblings settled down and Ethan

prowled toward Mari. Her pulse quickened as she regarded him curiously.

"You good?" Ethan asked.

Mari nodded. She couldn't remember the last time a man not related to her asked if she was okay.

"I'll be back in a few. I'm gonna shower really quick." He looked at his brother, then Jen. "You fill her in on the plan yet?"

"No, figured we'd wait on you."

"Good, though Jen could get to work on the legal stuff," Ethan commented. "We've got a meeting with the sketch artist later today. I'd like you there with us, sis. They aren't bleeding blue on her again."

Mari's heart thudded wildly as Ethan regarded her a moment then headed out of the room. She shifted her feet on the low rungs of the stool and looked at Jen. "I appreciate all the help, but I'm afraid I can't accept it. My finances are in dismal shape because of the divorce. I don't have the funds for an attorney."

"Which is why you need an attorney now more than ever," the woman said. "Your husband was an abuser. Those debts shouldn't be yours to incur, and they won't be when I'm done."

Mari choked as the shock rolled through her. How did the woman know Chester had abused her?

41

Milo offered her a glass of orange juice and held out a plate with an omelet and three strips of bacon. Her stomach rumbled as she accepted the plate and glass.

"You aren't alone in this fight anymore, Mari. Not by a long shot." Jen took a twin plate and steered Mari to the small dining room table within the breakfast nook. Unlike the rest of the furniture, the small eating surface was weathered with age and regular use.

"The fight's just begun," Milo commented. "Eat, then we'll chat."

Mari studied each scrape in the wood, wondering what stories the table could tell if it spoke. She'd always found the mysteries within beautiful pieces such as that one amazing. Her dad had always been fascinated with antiquing, and had taken her along whenever he could.

Dad. She knew she needed to call her parents, but they'd endured enough because of her. They deserved to enjoy Florida rather than worry about her.

She picked up her fork and focused on the task at hand—eat the omelet.

Mari was grateful for the silence as they ate. She was halfway through her omelet when Ethan returned. He took one of the plates Milo held out, and the two men sat at the small table. They offered duplicate smiles and got to eating.

Jen took a sip of her coffee, then deposited her plate on the bar behind her. She grabbed a legal pad from her briefcase, then sat back down. "Why don't we start with a brief history? How long were you together? How much of the abuse was documented? So far Beth and Tex have found a few records, but I'm thinking most of them didn't get saved."

"We dated six months and were married three years, two months and eighteen days." She let the fact she'd counted the days speak for itself since she was thinking happily married folk might not do that. "Documentation was a challenge, especially toward the end. He got smarter and smarter. My last attorney has copies of everything. Mine were stolen."

"Stolen?" Ethan asked.

"Break-in number one, two apartments ago."

"And the APD hasn't considered these break-ins might be something else?" Jen asked, her brows furrowed once more. "What's the attorney's name?"

"Oliver Winn and I don't know what, if anything, the APD considers. Honestly, I gave up on them getting this to stop a long time ago. As far as I can tell, they just think I'm the unluckiest person around."

"I see." Jenn's lips pinched together as she tapped her pen on a pad of paper. "And you have a restraining order. That's good. Have you had any issues with anyone within the APD specifically?"

"No, nothing abnormal," she admitted. "I know everyone there is likely above board. It's not their fault Chester was an abusive asshole. They're taking their fellow officer's back."

"Friends should be loyal, not blind," Ethan commented. He reached over and took her hand, squeezing it. "We've got enough contacts and resources to put a sizeable dent in that loyalty. I know you're drowning in all this, sweetheart, but we're here to get you to safe ground."

"Why are we talking about Chester, by the way?" She glanced around, noting the way Ethan and his brother looked at one another as the latter carried a couple plates to the table.

She knew last night was her ex's doing, but she hadn't told them.

He handed one off to Ethan and sat. "Twitch and a couple of the other guys took a look around your apartment and the complex after the APD left. We found a couple of interesting things."

Shady Apartments wasn't in the best neighborhood. The high legal bills had drained her bank accounts long ago. Then there was all the credit card debt Chester had managed to accumulate under their names. It'd taken her months to track down all the credit card companies and get the accounts shut down.

By then the damage had been done. She'd taken on a second job and worked her ass off, but she hadn't even made a dent in what she owed. She'd wallowed in the it's-not-fair pool the first few weeks, but it hadn't accomplished anything. Sure, she could file bankruptcy, but she wasn't raised to take the easy way out.

She may not have racked up the debt, but she'd married Chester. Every dollar she paid down to the shitstorm he'd left in his wake was a penance.

A second job helped keep her afloat long enough to have electricity and the basic necessities like groceries, but she had been sinking for the past few months. The decision to move yet again had been difficult, mainly because every move translated into more deposits and expense.

"It's all I could afford, and the last place wasn't an option, not any longer."

"And the last place was?" Jen asked.

"Las Colinas Meadows, on Slaughter."

"And you moved because of a break-in?" Milo asked.

"Yes, and my new neighbors were cops," she whispered, suddenly embarrassed about her decision to flee the nicer complex simply because two police officers moved in. "Some moved into the unit beside mine at the complex before Las Colinas, and that didn't go well. I filed several complaints with the APD about those officers because their conduct was...questionable."

"Good. Paper trails are critical when we can get them." Jen glanced at her brothers. "We'll get someone to look into the new neighbors at Las Colinas. Maybe a few undercover questions could help determine the sudden rash of officers taking up residence next door to Mari everywhere she moves. Once is random. Twice is strange."

"I got a new neighbor in 703 the day before yesterday," Mari said.

"Let me guess. APD?" Ethan's gaze cut over to his sister. "Three times is a problem I'm handling."

"No, third time's a problem *I'm* handling. I'm the one with the fancy law degree. You two handle fieldwork, while I fight red tape, politics, and all the other games people play." Jen glanced at Mari. "This is a good start, enough to get our teams investigating a few different things. Chester is done messing with you."

There it was again. Affirmation that Twitch and the other guys who'd looked around Shady Apartments found something they hadn't liked, something Jen and her brothers suspected Chester of. "What did you find?"

She'd gone enough rounds with her crazy ex to recognize him from two miles away in the dark. She'd recognize his punches, his hands. His breath.

Chester says hello, cunt. She forced back a shudder that rolled through her and took a sip of juice. But there was no flavor. Everything was metallic cardboard whenever she thought of the shit she'd endured because of Chester.

"There was a discarded photo of you in the trash bin nearest your unit. Your address and apartment number were on the back," Ethan said.

"We should set up an appointment with Internal Affairs," Milo said.

Mari tightened. Chester wouldn't take that well at all. She choked on the fear a few moments but didn't respond. For once she had someone else willing to tag in and handle the next bout. And that felt good.

Really, really good.

"You aren't surprised he's behind this," Jen commented. "I know it's difficult, and you don't know us or trust us yet, but we need to know everything, Mari. If something else happened last night, we need to know now rather than finding out about it later."

Damn.

She studied the other woman a moment. She was right. They'd already figured out Chester hired the guy. "The guy mentioned Chester by name when he was…"

A lump formed in her throat. The rest of the words wouldn't roll across her tongue. Her stomach churned.

"We have what we need," Jen said softly as she reached over and patted Mari's hand.

Ethan squeezed her arm. "It's going to be okay, Mari. We won't stop until we fix this for you."

The doorbell rang. Ethan and Milo looked at one another and rose.

"Stay here," Ethan ordered as he followed his brother into the other room.

Mari's pulse quickened. Her heart thudded against her chest. There was no reason to be concerned, but she was. Every knock, every ringing doorbell was another potential threat, another way Chester was messing with her mind.

"Come on," Jen said as she rose from her seat. "You aren't cowering in the corner, Mari. You did absolutely nothing wrong, and you've lost enough of your life because of that asshole. My brothers mean well, but Counterstrike is about more than keeping you and our other clients safe. It's about giving you the tools you need to help you stay that way. And the first tool for you is anger."

"I have plenty of that."

"Good. Then it's time you start honing it into a weapon, wielding it whenever your flight response kicks in. You're done running. From now on, you stand your ground and fight." Jen headed toward the entryway spilling into the living room. She paused. "Are you coming?"

Mari swallowed. She was right, but she was also wrong. "I fought, but I could only go so many rounds before I had to run."

She wasn't a kickass soldier like her brother, Ethan, and Milo. She wasn't a natural fighter. And she didn't even know who she was fighting anymore because the enemy was a faceless beast controlled by her ex. Interchangeable soldiers and incidents, one after another. She hadn't seen Chester in months, because he followed the restraining order to the very letter of the law.

But Jen was right. Mari had lost years of her life because of that bastard. She stood and followed the woman into the living room. And froze.

"Get back in the kitchen," Ethan ordered.

His gaze remained locked on the imposing man standing in the entryway of the house. A small woman with pink and purple-tipped hair stood beside him, not that Ethan and Milo appeared to notice her.

No, their gazes were locked on the man before them. Stance relaxed, he didn't appear phased in the slightest that Ethan and Milo seemed to be seconds away from kicking his ass.

The woman punched the man beside her. "Behave. I told you not to piss off Tex's friends."

Mention of the phantom Tex eased Ethan's and Milo's stances. The former reached out, snagged Mari and drew her behind him fully.

Yikes.

The stranger tracked the move with a smirk. He held out a hand. "Gage Sanderson, Arsenal. This is Zoey Dawson, Tex's friend, and the newest member of the Arsenal's nerd collective."

"Nerd collective? Seriously?" The woman shook

her head. "I swear you're one stupid statement away from me darting your ass."

The man chuckled. "Go ahead and try it, Little Bit."

"Don't mind him," the woman quipped. "We don't allow him to socialize much. I'm Zoey, but Tex knows me as Zero D. Sorry for the delay in getting here, but my bosses wanted to vet you all and your operation before they decided whether we would help or not."

"The last I heard, you were looking into the possibility, said you'd call Tex back," Ethan said, a slight growl in his voice. "There wasn't a discussion about you showing up."

"Right." The woman blinked, seemingly unfazed by his anger. "Jud and his nephew Jacob are at your headquarters. That didn't go well. You should call."

"Fuck," Milo replied as he dragged out his cell. He punched a button. A voice came on over the speaker.

"We're a little busy here right now, boss, but you might want to get your ass down here."

"Afraid that's not happening, Jet. Status?"

"Uh, yeah. Status. Everyone's a bit in shock, rattled and..." Jet sighed. "Field's assessing for injuries. So far everyone seems okay, except for Twitch. He's...down."

"Twitch is down?" Ethan glared at Gage. "What the hell did you do to our men?"

"I told you we should've handled headquarters," Zoey muttered. She sighed, set her duffel bag down, and trundled over to Milo like he wasn't pinning her with daggers via his gaze. She snagged his phone. "Give the phone to the lummox."

"Come again?"

"Give. The. Phone. To. The. Lummox." She sighed. "You know, the guy who just plowed through all of you."

"Who the hell is this?" Jet demanded.

"Jet," Milo said, his lips thinned. "They're friends of Tex's, or so we're being told. Do what she says."

"I'll hand the phone over to the runt. I'm not going near the other bastard."

"Jacob is not a runt. He's twenty! He's got at least one more growth spurt ahead of him, if not two," Zoey spewed angrily into the phone.

"Z," a voice said. "Uncle Jud tried to be nice. Honest. But Twitch was bigger than we expected and didn't take it too kindly when we didn't leave like he ordered. I don't think he was used to someone refusing him anything."

"Please tell me Jud didn't hurt anyone."

"Nah, everyone's good, but Uncle Jud and Twitch are a little pissed at me. They wouldn't stop fighting, and it was agitating everyone else, so I zinged them both."

Zoey blinked. Eyes wide, she stammered, "You what?"

"I had a couple of the drones out, the ones armed with zingers. I was surveying the building like Quillery and Edge wanted. So when they wouldn't stop, I zinged them."

"Them?" Gage asked, his voice lilted with humor.

"Yeah, Uncle Jud and the other guy. The brick mountain."

"Twitch," Milo supplied.

"Please tell me you have that footage," Zoey said with a grin. "I can't believe you tasered Judson Jensen."

"Uncle Jud isn't very happy right now. I should get back to him and the other guy before they wake up." The voice halted. "What's up?"

"Give the phone back to Jet. His bosses need confirmation everyone's okay, then we can move on. Tell Jud to behave."

"Right."

Zoey turned the phone back over to Milo and

looked at Mari. She visibly paled and stumbled on her high heels. Gage reached out and leaned her against his tall, muscular frame.

"Who did that to you?" The woman glared at Ethan. "Tex told me you needed a security system. He told me you all were helping a friend with a *sticky situation*. Cracked ribs and an asshole ex with a badge. He didn't mention a busted face. That isn't a *sticky situation*."

Mari gulped and edged closer to Ethan.

"Who did that to you?" Zoey repeated, her voice harder than before.

"We're finding out, though her ex is likely behind it."

"Right." Zoey pinned Mari with another intense gaze.

"Dial it back a notch, Little Bit. You're scaring her," Gage whispered.

Zoey clicked something in her ear. "We're either in, or I'm in, and you really don't want me handling this without it being an Arsenal decision. One way or another, I'm not leaving until Counterstrike has the tools they need to help her out of this *sticky situation*."

Yowza.

Gage's gaze narrowed as he looked at Zoey, then

reached up and hit something in his ear. "Sorry, ladies, I'm with Z on this one."

Zoey's eyes widened as she peered up at the man like he'd suddenly grown two heads.

"No, I know," Zoey said into the com. "Right. Of course. Erm...did you miss the part where your man almost got pummeled by one of their guys? 'Cause I didn't even see it, and I know that's evidence enough they can handle securing whatever we give them."

Silence ticked by as Zoey and Gage listened to what Mari assumed was the other side of a conversation. Every second that ticked by raised her pulse a notch. Ethan settled an arm around her.

"Okay, good. Okay, okay, okay, I'm good." Zoey expended a long breath. "Right. I'll coordinate with Gemini. I know you two are the badasses with the brains and the strategic minds, but this is my wheelhouse. I'm point on the safehouses."

The woman clicked off, then looked at Ethan. "Vi and Mary agreed to install a security system into all Counterstrike facilities. We're doing your house here, Jen's next door, and your headquarters today. We've got six teams en route to begin on your twelve safehouses first thing in the morning. We need to coordinate their work to not frighten or disturb anyone who might be there."

Mari noted the tension in Ethan's stance as he glanced at his brother.

"Vi and Mary? The kid on the phone mentioned Quillery and Edge."

"Yeah. That's their codenames," Zoey replied. Her eyes widened. "Oh, wow. That's my bad. Okay, Edge, calm down. Yeesh, Jacob didn't know. The pieces barely clicked for me, and I memorized all the files on the way up here."

"What am I missing?" Mari asked.

"Nolan Mason and his brothers run the Arsenal, where these two are from," Ethan said. "He saved my life in the jungle, kept me alive."

"Okay," Jen said, her voice low.

Mari took Ethan's hand and squeezed, not sure what about that had made him react.

"The Edge was the voice on the com, the one who talked him through what to do, kept him focused on keeping his team safe. Me alive."

CHAPTER 4

FIRST NOLAN MASON. NOW THE EDGE. THE SPEC OPS world was a small one, but Ethan didn't realize how much so until a few hours ago when he'd heard Jacob reference the Quillery Edge.

He wasn't sure what to think about their paths crossing once again, so he packed the thought away to focus on another time. For now, he was single-mindedly determined to make Mari's world safer.

The first step in that mission was her statement about the break-in and assault. He squeezed her hand as they followed Detective Raul Rodriguez into a small room with a sofa along one wall and a chair on the other. A camera pointed down at the two seating places.

"I'd rather you step outside, wait for Ms. Santos

there. We have coffee around the corner in a break-room," Detective Rodriguez commented.

"I'd rather he stay," Mari replied quickly.

Ethan's protective instincts ratcheted up a couple notches when she squeezed his hand harder. He sat beside her on the sofa and dared the detective to do anything about it. If she wanted him there, he wasn't leaving.

The detective's lips quirked up in a grin. "Tex said you were stubborn."

Ethan didn't offer comment. Just because he knew Tex didn't make him good people, it just made him smart.

"I'm going to share a couple things with you, Ms. Santos, because I feel it's important we start our relationship off on the right foot." The detective motioned toward the cameras. "A couple acquaintances of mine are working with the Internal Affairs Division to investigate your ex-husband. I've been asked to facilitate information gathering from you on their behalf."

Holy crap.

"It's unfortunate my presence here is because you suffered yet another incident. I assure you as far as my acquaintances and I are concerned, it'll be the last." Detective Rodriguez looked at Ethan. "From what Tex has told me, your operation is the best around. I agree. We've heard a lot of great things about Counterstrike. Hell, a lot of the cases I've worked have crossed your path at one point or another."

"I'm not here because of last night." Mari tensed against Ethan. Her voice was low, pained. "You don't care about last night."

Ethan wrapped an arm around her and wished he could take away her pain, undo what'd happened to put it there. She trembled but relaxed within his hold.

"I am most certainly taking a statement about last night's attack, Ms. Santos. I do care, more than you'll likely ever know. No one gets by with hurting anyone on my watch." The detective leaned forward. "But this isn't the first time you've had trouble. I've looked into your previous incidents. Things are escalating. It's time someone got to the root of the real problem and dug it out of your life. It'll be my pleasure helping that happen. So in that respect, I'm not focused on last night. I'm focused on why it happened in the first place. That's why you're here."

"W-what do I need to do?"

"Take a deep breath," the man advised. "We'll start at the beginning whenever you're ready."

Ethan sat back and studied the man a moment. Pieces clicked together in his head. "I'm thinking Tex didn't wait for my say to get a certain friend of ours in the Texas Rangers activated."

Raul's eyebrows rose. "I'm not at liberty to discuss an ongoing investigation, but I can assure you all pertinent outside agencies have been in contact with the Internal Affairs Division and the investigation is being taken very seriously."

Ethan and Milo had met Daxton Chambers a couple months after starting Counterstrike, when their first client's troubles necessitated Tex's involvement. Chambers, along with a couple buddies of his from the San Antonio Police Department had helped get their client's mother secure when a drug dealer had threatened her life.

Daxton Chambers was one hell of an officer, as was all the others he'd met through Tex. The fact they were a short trip down Interstate 35 in San Antonio was reassuring. He'd intended to phone Dax, get his input on how best to proceed with this situation once he got a firmer grasp on the details.

Clearly things were progressing faster than Ethan expected, likely because of the whirlwind known as Zoey who'd entered the situation. Tex's friend was a touch strange, but Ethan couldn't deny that she, Gage, Jacob and Jud had gotten to work immediately.

His mind wandered to Nolan Mason, but Ethan shoved the thoughts aside. Everything else would have to wait until he got Mari secured. All that mattered right now was helping her through giving her statement.

MARI SWALLOWED THE UNEASE RISING IN HER THROAT as Ethan navigated his massive truck into a narrow parking spot of the unpaved parking lot. She stared at the green dumpster beside the vehicle as her heart thudded in her chest.

Her gaze swept upward until it rested on the small eatery in a small out-of-the-way pocket of East Austin. Hank's was a downhome style restaurant that was more of a local watering hole for cops, firefighters and every other assortment of first responders than anything else.

"Why are we here?" She forced the words out even though she already knew the answer.

"Look at me, Mari." Ethan's firm voice drew her focus.

She blinked, turned her head and tumbled into

the light cinnamon-swirled gaze. "This isn't a good idea."

"He's done messing with you," Ethan declared. "We walk in there, your face looking like a punching bag, everyone in his crew will get wind of what went down. You do it with me and my crew at your back, they'll know things have changed."

She swallowed. Shame kept her silent. He made it sound so simple. Maybe for him it was. She'd tried. She'd fought, both inside and outside court for so long. It wasn't like she wasn't prepared to go another twenty rounds with Chester, because she was. She just wasn't an in-your-face style fighter.

"We're sending a message, a warning to everyone in blue to either do the right thing, or stay the hell out of our way while we take out the trash," Ethan continued. "You're what matters in this situation, Mari. If you aren't ready to walk in there, then we'll go back to the house."

The offer was sweet, but the firm set to Ethan's jaw as his gaze slid over to the entrance of Hank's spoke volumes. And he was right. Walking in there with her face bruising from the latest episode of her Chester nightmare was the right move, even if it felt like the most terrifying thing she'd ever done.

For the first time in a long while she'd left a

police station feeling safe. Detective Rodriguez had been professional, kind and considerate. He'd been patient. He'd let her stop and take a break whenever she wanted, which she'd done more than once. Composing herself in the bathroom gave her small breaks from the intensity within the room, which had spiked incrementally as she offered more insight into what all she'd endured since the divorce proceedings began.

The questions had been intense, pointed and very embarrassing in so many ways, but she'd passed the point of worrying about what people thought about her long ago. She had very few, if any, real friends. They'd vacated her life like rats fleeing a sinking ship.

A couple of them called periodically, but the infrequent visits felt more like an interrogation than a friendly outing. It wasn't until Christina's last visit that she'd finally accepted what was going on—they were trolling her for gossip. The hell Mari endured was nothing more than fodder for their little clique of friends.

And most of Chester's friends were cops, who drank and hung out at Hank's.

Her stomach churned.

"Mari." Ethan caressed her cheek with the pad of

his thumb. The slow, methodical strokes dragged her away from the riotous what-ifs running amuck in her brain.

The thoughts slowed, her focus narrowed to the gentle glide across her skin. She focused on discerning the languid patterns he formed.

M. Her pulse quickened, not from fear, but awareness.

A. Gods, the man was lethal to her senses.

R. A gasp escaped her as she shifted her gaze to his face. A slow grin spread across his handsome face. She swallowed.

Ethan's thumb froze at the seam of her lips, right at the edge. She licked her lips, watched his gaze track the swipe of her tongue. Heat spiraled through her as his thumb swept across her lower cheek, then halfway back and up. Her heart thudded in her chest. Breath held, she anticipated the stroke left across her upper cheek.

But he went right as the lazy grin on his face deepened to a knowing smile she felt clear to her toes. Left, all the way, and then back to the right where she'd expected.

I.

Ethan leaned in until his hot breath feathered

across the cheek he'd just spelled her name out on. "Breathe for me, sweetheart."

Heat crawled through her as she obeyed and peered into his intense gaze. For the first time in a long, long while she wasn't the ex-wife of an abusive cop. She wasn't a hopeless debtor in over her head.

Vanilla mingled with pine when she inhaled deep. The scent permeated her nostrils, infused with the heat radiating from Ethan. She reached out and stroked his face where he'd touched her.

"They can't touch you, Mari. You hold the power, and whatever they do will bounce right off you as long as you remember you are not alone. You are not the cause, the blame, or the guilty party in this."

"I'm the victim," she whispered.

"Victim is not in your vocabulary. Ever. No woman who takes on the fight you've waged is anything but a victor. A survivor." He caressed her other cheek. "They can't touch you, Mari, because the second they try, I'll make them wish they were never born."

As if sensing she couldn't find the words to respond, he continued. "So will everyone in there waiting for us. This is a statement, but you aren't the only one making it."

Her eyes burned as she pulled back enough to

look into his eyes again. "I won't ever be able to repay Tex for bringing you into my life. For the first time since this started, I'm starting to think I might be close to the other side."

"You're still in deep, but you aren't alone. We'll get you to the other side," he promised. "We'd better get inside before I do something Milo and Jen would kick my ass for."

Awareness beaded along her skin. He felt the attraction, too? She nodded her head as she forced the thought aside. She had enough on her plate without adding a new relationship into the mix. No way in hell could she put anyone in Chester's crosshairs by dating him.

Ethan could handle Chester easily enough more than likely, but Mari didn't want to stir up any more trouble. She had nothing to offer a man like Ethan Davenport. She was in debt up to her eyeballs, and so far from dating material it wasn't funny.

Which meant she needed to get the heck out of his truck before she did something impulsive. She licked her lips, savoring the shot of awareness when he did the same with his.

"Wait until I come around to get out," he said.

Then he was out of the truck fast enough to leave her mind reeling. She gave herself a moment to accept the fact she was about to walk into Hank's and have a beer and a meal like it wasn't a cop hang-out, like she hadn't done their entire world wrong by divorcing one of theirs.

Her face throbbed where she'd been punched. The achy reminder was exactly what she needed to keep her centered on the task at hand—standing her ground.

She unbuckled her seatbelt as Ethan opened the door. He gripped her hips firmly when she turned around. A startled gasp escaped her when he lifted her out of the truck like it wasn't a big deal. She weighed a good thirty pounds more than she should, if not more.

Mortification heated her cheeks as she averted her gaze away from him. A man like him definitely deserved more than a frumpy, disheveled, fat ex-wife of an asshole cop. She clutched the thought firmly as he put his arm around her and pressed her fully against his side until the heat wafting from his body seeped into her.

Protected.

She clung to the sensation until the tremble in her hands lessened. Ethan wasn't going to let them mess with her. And, really...

What more could they do?

Country music played softly in the background, the distinctive twang barely discernible above the buzz of conversations echoing within the small restaurant. A long L-shaped bar took up the entire right side.

Ethan angled them to the left and into the thick of the eatery like he'd been there a thousand times. An older gentleman stepped into their path. Hank.

Mari had met the man plenty of times when she'd been with Chester. Time hadn't been good to him the last few months. His hair was more salt than pepper now, and more wrinkles creased his brow. Large bags sagged beneath his eyes, eyes which always seemed to pierce straight into her.

"Hank," she said by way of greeting.

"Whatever your play is, it's not smart. You'd best turn around and head on home, Marisol. This is a hornet's nest you don't want to be kicking."

"She won't be the one kicking," Ethan declared.

"What business is it of yours, Davenport?" Hank asked. "You and your brother have my respect. We soldiers stick together, no matter what. But this mess with her and Chester has no business airing itself in my place."

"I'm thinking you know it's past time the truth aired itself where Marisol is concerned," Ethan said.

"He's done messing with her unless he wants to take on Counterstrike."

"He's a good man," Hank argued.

A part of Mari locked down with the gritty determination radiating in the man's voice. Why couldn't anyone else see the monster behind the mask?

"Is that so?" Ethan edged closer. "You and I've dug up our bones over beers together enough for me to respect you, Hank. The things you did, the sacrifices you made. You've earned my respect. And my brother's. You bleed red, white and blue just like we do. Don't let that blue choke out your brain."

Hank's gaze swept toward Mari and pinned her, much like a bug on a pin. Although she wanted to cower behind Ethan's body, she stood her ground at his side. Established eye contact with the man and waited as the silence ticked by.

An uncomfortable hush fell over the interior, but Mari ignored it and kept her attention on Hank. His stubble-covered jaw moved a couple times before he spoke.

"He do that?"

"No," she said honestly. "Someone broke into my place, attacked me. Third break-in since the divorce."

"Girl, that place isn't safe," the man admonished.

"Seems like you would've learned that after the first break-in. Didn't your momma give you any sense?"

"Yeah, she did, which was why I moved out of the first apartment into another after the first break-in. And again after the second. I'm done running," she said.

"You need a man in your life and in your bed. No one would mess with you if you had a man," Hank said.

"I'm still drowning from the last one. I'm not about to weigh myself down with another."

"Is that so?" Hank chuckled. "I'm thinking Davenport here might be disagreeing. He's mighty protective of you."

"Good men like him don't sit on their ass drinking beers and ignoring women getting beaten and terrified by their asshole exes that can't move the hell on." She let her voice rise as she spoke so everyone could hear what she said. Ethan was right.

It was time to make a stand.

"Nothing he ever did was good enough for you. Don't think I'll sit here and let you trash talk him." A chair scraped.

Mari's gaze swept toward the sound, but she couldn't see the speaker as three tables of people rose between her and the speaker. She gulped at the mountain of muscle. She recognized Milo and Gage, but there were at least twenty more. They took up the entire center of the restaurant.

Mari closed the distance between herself and the speaker. Ethan grabbed at her arm, but she was focused on her quarry. Of course. Roger Hamits. He was in the same division as Chester. Likely he'd had more than a few bullshit stories fed to him.

"You're right, Roger." She waited for her statement to settle in the room. "Nothing he ever did was good enough for me. I guess I should've been okay with getting hit so hard I got a concussion, all because he chose to come here and hang out with you all for two hours and didn't tell me. How dare I not accept that and let dinner burn. Burned chicken parmesan's deserving of a concussion, huh?"

"That was self-defense," Roger argued. "You came at him first."

"Oh?" She crossed her arms and let the anger take over. Jen was right. Anger was an awesome starting point to a new front on this war. "So an armed detective, one of Austin's finest, has no recourse against a five-foot-two, unarmed woman but to batter her to the point of a concussion? Repeatedly?"

She let that statement thunder through the room

71

a moment, then continued. "Fine. I'll give you that. I suppose I deserved what I got for not being a perfect, mind-reading chef. That's sarcasm by the way, Roger. I'm not sure if you and everyone else in here gets that, so I'll be really clear. I was not okay with him beating me when dinner got cold while he was drinking away his paycheck in this dump."

The man's face reddened. Someone behind her chuckled.

"Oh, and I was definitely not okay with him doing our neighbor," she admitted. "In our bed. That earned me a couple punches, too, because I dared to come home early. I guess I should've been okay with that, too, huh?"

Anger churned into rage as she took a step forward and continued her verbal assault on Chester's friend. She was tired of cowering around them. "You disgust me, Roger. Every last one of you so-called protectors of the innocent. You're nothing but hypocritical, sanctimonious sacks of shit as far as I'm concerned because you'll protect and serve as long as it serves your personal agenda. You think you're above the law because as far as you're concerned, you are the law."

Roger put a hand on his belt. A growl rumbled from behind Mari, but she kept her focus on the asshole before her. He and all the others who'd ignored the hell she'd been enduring.

For years.

"Jud, no," a female voice said. "This is a no-body-bag night. Ethan and his men have this covered."

And they did. Mari took a deeper breath when she realized she wasn't alone. More importantly, Roger knew. Which meant Chester would hear soon enough.

"He's done messing with me, Roger," Mari said. "I've swallowed enough of his bullshit while you and everyone else hired to protect people like me looked the other way. Or helped him. You're all done messing with me."

"Is that a threat?" Roger asked.

"It's a warning I'd heed," Ethan replied. "Mess with her and you mess with Counterstrike. Make sure your buddy gets the message."

"I think this conversation's over," Hank declared. Arms crossed, he looked at Roger. "Sit down or get out."

"She came in here to stir up trouble. I won't have her or anyone else talking trash about Chester behind his back. None of us will."

"Take a look around you," Ethan advised. "You

are the only one standing up having words with her."

And he was. Mari's gaze swept the restaurant. While everyone watched, no one else had added their presence to the discussion. Either they suddenly believed her story, or they didn't want to mess with Ethan and the twelve other people standing around her. Emotion clogged her throat.

She hadn't had people at her back in this fight since...ever. She turned and shifted her focus to the three tables of people who'd all stood and positioned themselves between her and Roger. All the men were tall, muscular, and not very pleased if the expressions on their faces were any indication.

No one moved to sit, not even after Roger skulked back to his booth along the back wall. She gulped. Now what?

"We good?" Ethan asked, his gaze locked on Hank, whose regard remained locked on Mari.

"Far from it. I'm thinking I got choked out by the blue a while back," the man admitted. He looked at Ethan. "It won't happen again. This is a safe haven, for her, or anyone else your crew's helping. Whatever you need, whenever. Let me know."

"Appreciated," Milo said from Mari's other side.

"Someone'll be over to get your orders,' Hank said as he shuffled away.

Mari released the breath she hadn't realized she held. Her agitated pulse beat its fury in her ears, but the knots in her stomach had loosened. Had she...

Had she actually won a skirmish in the war with her ex?

She honestly wasn't sure. He wasn't here, but he may as well have been. Hank's was so filled with his buddies in blue the atmosphere was thick with tension. Even though no one had risen to take Roger's back, they'd all been tuned to the confrontation. They'd heard.

And said nothing.

"What's wrong, sweetheart?" Ethan's hot breath against her neck and his hand at her hip felt right. Good.

"Nothing," she answered honestly. "I didn't think it'd go that well."

"It went well because of you, Mari. You stood your ground and gave them a heaping dose of truth, one so big it was likely hard to swallow," Ethan said. "I'm proud of you. I know that wasn't easy, but it was necessary."

The reality of what she'd done seeped into her, an unwelcomed douse of unease. "He'll react."

75

When Ethan's eyebrows lifted, she continued. "Chester. He'll react."

"Good. That's what we want."

"You don't know what he's capable of."

"And you don't know what we're capable of," he returned. "Trust me and trust my guys. This isn't your fight any longer. It's ours, and we've fought worst assholes than Chester."

They may have, but Ethan was wrong. "This is still my fight. You may have tagged in, but I'm still in it. I'm not cowering in the corner while you take over."

Ethan ran a hand down her hair. Intensity reflected on his handsome face when he looked her in the eyes. "I'd never expect you to sit on the sidelines of your own battle, especially one you've fought so long, Mari. You're one hell of a woman. I may not have known you for long, but I recognize the strength it's taken to endure this as long as you have. And I admire the hell out of you. Just because we've tagged in doesn't mean we expect you to tag out."

"Good," she replied, unsure what else there was to say.

"Let's eat," Milo said. "I'm starving."

"You're always starving," one of the men said with a chuckle as he sat at the table.

Mari sat between Ethan and Milo and smiled as the gathered group bantered back and forth. Their ease with one another was apparent.

A team.

One now fighting for her.

She glanced across the table at the pink and purple-haired woman who wore a big grin on her face. Zoey. "I like you."

"Thanks," Mari said, a little wary because the woman was seriously intense.

"You stood your ground just now. That's good. Guys like Ethan go from quiet to lethal in less than a second. You ever need advice on how to handle that, you give me a ring. My girls and I will help you out."

"Stay out of her shit," a man growled beside Zoey. She's got enough troubles without you adding to it."

The woman glared. "Careful, Jud. We still have zingers. I'll knock you out again, teach you a few manners."

"He's right. She's got enough on her plate without you dragging her into the fold," Gage said.

"And exactly how would my dragging her into the fold add trouble?" The woman paused. Gage's brows shot up. Her eyes widened. "Okay, never mind. I see your point."

The man smirked and glanced at Mari. "She's right, though. Whatever you need, whenever. The Arsenal will help. You and Counterstrike."

"The Arsenal?" Mari asked.

"You'll meet everyone tomorrow, or most everyone," Jud said. "A hell of a group, but it looks like you've already got one behind you. Still, it never hurts to have another in queue in case shit hits the fan faster or harder than expected."

"Tex has their back," Zoey said. "But the lummox is right. Whatever you and your crew need, Ethan, we'll help however we can. Tex is great, and I know Beth is, too, but Quillery, Edge and I are available. You and I will talk one-on-one before I leave."

"Leave him be, Little Bit," Gage suggested.

"It's not any of your business," the woman shot back.

"Like hell it isn't. I was sent along with specific orders to keep you wrangled. Until we get back to the compound, you are my only business."

Jud chuckled. "Good luck with that, man. I'm thinking my woman's attitude is rubbing off on Z."

CHAPTER 5

"There's plenty of room here," Milo offered.

Ethan gnashed his teeth and tried not to glare at his brother. While the meal at Hank's had gone well and he'd enjoyed hanging out with his teammates and getting to know The Arsenal crew, he didn't want Zoey, Gage, Jud, and Jacob crashing at the house.

Not with Mari there. Ethan glanced down at the cat, who'd crawled from behind the sofa and was now winding her way around his feet.

"We're good," Zoey said. "Oh my God! What an adorable kitty. What's her name?"

"June Bug," Mari offered. "She's a rescue kitty."

"Oh, that's awesome. I have a cutie myself named Dobie."

"Cute is a very loose term," Gage muttered. Zoey growled and scratched June Bug's head.

"We've secured a rental nearby. If there's trouble, the system is queued to warn us. It's a safety precaution until you're fully trained on how to use it."

From what Twitch and Milo indicated, the system was beyond slick. "We appreciate all the help."

"No thanks necessary," Gage replied. "Let's get out of their hair, Little Bit. He needs to get Mari secured in the house."

Ethan glanced around the quiet neighborhood. While they'd never had troubles, they hadn't gone toe-to-toe with an APD officer before. Backlash was possible. He placed a protective hand on Mari's back as Zoey shoved a laptop at Gage and approached them.

"Here's my cell number. Whenever you need something, you let me know," the woman whispered. Her gaze settled on Ethan. "Tex is good, but I'm more capable of helping with certain situations. Gage and the others aren't fully versed in what I do outside The Arsenal. I can help with what you do here. If you ever need someone hidden where they'll never be found, call. I can and will permanently ghost anyone in twenty-four hours, less if necessary. What you're doing here is good. You ever need money, let me know. Quillery is good at finding deep pockets of sick assholes."

"Tex has us covered," Ethan said, not bothering to mention Davenport pockets were plenty deep thanks to the old man. It was likely the woman already knew because he couldn't imagine any operation Tex considered the best around not looking into him and everyone at Counterstrike. "We'll see you in the morning."

Zoey, Gage, and Jacob headed toward a black SUV parked at the curb. Jud hung back. His gaze swept toward the tree line along the edge of Ethan's property.

Ethan's insides tightened as a shadow shifted. He firmed his contact on Mari as he regarded the man who'd kicked Twitch's ass. The man's gaze slid to Mari, then to the house.

Right. Whatever, no whoever, awaited him in the shadows had nothing to do with her. Ethan knew the shadow's identity. Nolan Mason.

"You good?" Milo asked.

"Take Mari inside. I'll be in shortly," Ethan said.

Big brother by two minutes slid his attention to the shadowed figure. "Right. Five minutes, then I'm coming out."

"Ethan? Is everything okay?" Mari asked, her voice pitched higher than normal.

"It's fine, sweetheart. I need to talk to someone. It's not about Chester, or your situation. Everything's fine."

"Oh, okay." Mari looked at Jud. "I-It was a pleasure to meet you."

The man smiled but offered no comment otherwise as he shuffled toward the truck. Ethan waited until Milo had Mari inside the house before he closed the distance between himself and Nolan Mason.

His gut clenched as a burn began where his gut wound had been. Some nights the phantom pain and memories were harder to fight off than others. Hell, some days were even harder. Night terrors had stopped a few years ago, but he still had residual nightmares, flashes of hell that seared into his memories.

But at least he was alive.

Thanks to Nolan.

The man shifted from the shadows as Ethan halted just within the fringes of the living room window's periphery vision. He didn't want Mari or Milo worrying unnecessarily. He sure as hell didn't want big brother coming outside.

"We didn't get a chance to formally meet last time," the man said as he held out a hand. "Nolan, though most knew me by No."

Ethan clasped the man's hand and dragged him into a back-slapping, half hug. Some of the tightness within him eased. "I should've hunted you and your team down long ago."

"Most of us are out at The Arsenal now, though a couple decided to enjoy a well-deserved civilian life." Nolan glanced at the house. "Hell of a setup you have here. Quillery and Edge were both impressed with Counterstrike. Your teams."

Edge. Ethan looked around. While meeting Nolan tonight rather than tomorrow while everyone was about was good, the woman who'd rescued them all was another story. He'd heard enough through the years about the Quillery Edge. They were a force no one messed with.

"She's at the rental house. We got in a little bit ago," Nolan offered. He held out a roll of papers. "Tentative plans for the morning. Twitch forwarded what we needed in the way of which locations were in use and which were empty. Look over what we've devised when you can, let us know if it'll work."

Ethan took the roll of plans and nodded. "Appreciate the help, the system. Tex mentioned it was the best around."

"Yeah, I've gotta admit it still freaks the hell out of me sometimes." Nolan laughed. "They left most of the system intact on what we're installing, but the weaponry is very tamed down, and the automatic facial recognition scanning isn't active. There's more, but it's above my head. The women will run through it all tomorrow."

"Patch is our computer guru. He, Twitch and Milo can sit in on the information session," Ethan said. "I..."

"You've got a woman to secure," Nolan said. "I didn't want tomorrow to be about us meeting for the first time since..."

"Not a day goes by that I don't thank God, Fate, or whoever it was that put you in my path. You saved my life. No words can express my gratitude."

"You would've done the same."

"You lost a man getting me out. That's bound to cut deep."

"And you lost your entire team. I'm thinking that cuts deeper." The man glanced at the house. "You've got a hell of a crew. A family. I know a thing or two about that."

Ethan chuckled. "I've heard about you and your brothers. Big family, even bigger crew."

"We've all got our own dark. We keep it to ourselves, chew on it, let it chew on us," Nolan commented. "There comes a time where you have to drag that shit out into the light and give it over to someone else. Otherwise you'll lose yourself in the dark."

Ethan's jaw twitched as he looked away. He admired the hell out of Nolan Mason and his team for saving him, but he wasn't about to stand outside his home and get a lecture. Fortunately, the man must've sensed as much.

"We've got a program out at The Arsenal to help warriors work their way back to normal. It's not an easy road, but you'll get there. You need help, you know where we're at." Nolan motioned toward the house. "Best medicine is in that house. A strong family, an even stronger woman at your side. No better cure."

"She's a client," Ethan said. "Nothing more."

"Attraction is a finicky bitch. It strikes when it wants to. Best survival technique is to not resist. Gage and Jud both said she's a hell of a woman."

"Getting emotionally attached to our charges is a bad idea."

"Doesn't mean it doesn't happen," Nolan said with a grin. "We'll catch up tomorrow, after the work is done. There's been talk of grabbing Salt Lick barbecue and relaxing the evening away."

Ethan couldn't imagine much better than kicking back with a few cold beers, some great barbecue and getting to know the man who'd saved his life. Everyone at Counterstrike needed a few hours to relax. The lack of a good security system had put them all on edge for too long.

"I should've replaced those shitty systems long ago," he admitted.

"I heard they were installed by a friend of your mom's. Setting aside familial connections is tough. I've been there," Nolan said.

Mom. The thought poked Ethan's chest hard. He, Milo, and Jen had worked out a visitation schedule, but it often got waylaid by day-to-day life. Truth told, it still hurt like hell to see the woman who'd raised him...

He shoved the thought aside. It hurt too bad, burned too deep to let simmer tonight. Meeting Nolan Mason was enough of a fire to stoke tonight. "Come in, have a beer. Meet my brother."

"Tomorrow," the man replied with a smile. "I'd

best get back or my brothers will be out looking for me."

Ethan knew a thing or two about protective siblings. He glanced over at the porch and chuckled when he saw Jen hovering there. Very little flew beneath her radar.

He and Nolan exchanged a couple more back-slaps. Ethan headed toward the house as soon as Nolan's truck pulled away. Jen cut him off at the steps.

"Who was he?"

"Nolan Mason."

Her eyebrows furrowed. While he'd mentioned the name a few times to Milo, he hadn't ever shared it with Jen. Neither of them shared much about their military pasts with her.

"He and his team rescued me," he said.

"And he's with The Arsenal? Small world."

"The paramilitary arena he's in is very small. Elite. He and his brothers run The Arsenal."

"He should've come inside."

"You'll meet him and everyone else tomorrow, sis. Assuming we aren't busy with something else."

"I have a meeting with the Chief of Police tomorrow. And the District Attorney."

Ethan smiled and ruffled her hair. "You couldn't

let the dust settle a couple days before you stirred everyone up?"

"She's not waiting any longer than necessary. Her nightmare's lasted too long as it is," Jen said, her cheeks red within the pale porch light.

Ethan glanced at the door. As much as he wanted to chat with Jen, he wanted to be inside checking on Mari. Talking to her. The attraction was almost unbearable. He'd spoken the truth to Nolan earlier.

He and Milo had discussed Counterstrike's unofficial rule number one back when they'd formed the organization. The clients they protected relied on them. A unique relationship of trust and necessity was formed, a bond that would not be broken easily.

One which made taking advantage of a woman too simple.

Ethan wasn't a conceited ass, but he knew he was attractive. He'd run through more than his fair share of beautiful women back in the service. Now? Well, now he didn't give much of a damn if anyone shared his bed. He'd seen the byproduct of what happened when a relationship went bad.

He'd always assumed he'd be single forever. Settling down seemed foolish. Divorce was too prevalent. Marriage was a joke. They'd learned that the hard way growing up.

But a part of him still clung to the hope of finding a good woman and having a couple kids. Jesus. Where the hell had that come from?

It'd crept into his thoughts a lot lately. Maybe that was why the attraction to Mari was harder to resist than usual. No, there was something about her that roused the baser part of his nature. But he wouldn't act on it.

Mari deserved the time she needed to get back to normal. She deserved the fresh start he could ensure, which meant any attraction he had to her would have to wait. If it still lingered after they dealt with her asshole ex, then Ethan would see if she was interested.

Chester says hello, cunt.

Mari knifed out of bed as a scream rose from her throat. Sweat dampened her face and body as she kicked the sheets wrapped around her. She flailed her arms as she thudded to a halt on the ground beside the bed.

Sheets.

The bed.

She wasn't kicking a man off her. It was a sheet.

Arms weren't holding her down as he bit her breasts. Breaths sawed in and out of her lungs as her heart thundered wildly within her chest. She blinked, forced her attention to the surroundings slowly seeping into her awareness.

A shaft of pale light streamed into the room from a crack in the doorway. A shadow shifted as the door opened. Her pulse quickened.

Ethan prowled into the room, his bare feet striking the floor with no sound. She tracked his progression from her position on the floor with avid curiosity, much like a frozen gazelle in a lion's eyesight.

But he was no lion. No. He was...

Stunning.

The pale light from outside spilled across him as he moved deeper into the room and closer to her. Her mind still drifted between her nightmare and reality. She forced a deep breath despite the pain along her side.

"Mari, you're safe." His deep voice boomed within the otherwise silent night around her. She shifted within the sheet trapping her into place. He shuffled to a stop a couple feet away from her and looked down.

His full, thick lips upturned into a slight smirk

bordering on a smile. Warmth seeped into her and burned up her cheeks as she peered up at him. He was magnificent.

A scattering of hairs arrowed downward, bypassing a mottled mess of skin. A wound. She studied the injury for a breath or two. Then her gaze continued its meander down his bare chest. Rippling muscle and washboard abs. Her mouth dried as her perusal shifted to the drawstring dangling from his shorts—shorts which hugged his thick thighs very nicely. Shorts that accentuated…

Wowza.

"It looks like you're tangled up," he commented.

Right. Mari ignored the gorgeous man and the distinctive bulge her attention had honed in on moments ago. She wrestled with the sheet, but it'd snared her fully. Great.

Ethan chuckled as he crouched down. Humor danced within his eyes as he reached out and gently extricated her from the sheet. "I guess we should've left you with a KA-BAR to cut your way out."

"It would've been appreciated," she muttered.

Heat trailed where his fingers grazed. Tiny goosebumps marched along her arm as he slowly pried the unwanted obstruction from her. His gaze narrowed as his jaw twitched. She looked down and swallowed.

Bite marks.

Though most of them were hidden by her thin chemise top, a couple marred the swell of her breasts. At least most of the bruising was hidden. She'd noted their presence forming earlier before she'd gone to bed. A handprint. Which she'd dutifully, and quite numbly, snapped a pic of and sent it to the number she'd been given.

Revulsion rolled through her, but she fought it back.

The bastard had tried to break her.

Chester had sent him.

She'd fought him off and now she was safe.

At Ethan's.

Ethan wouldn't let it happen again. She wasn't sure how she knew that, but she did. Perhaps it was because her brother trusted Tex, and Tex trusted Ethan. Perhaps it was because Ethan and Milo and so many of their team were a lot like Joseph.

Soldiers.

No.

Spec ops soldiers.

There was a distinction, one she'd picked up on over the years. She didn't pretend to understand the military world, but she knew there were levels of badass. From what she'd gathered? Well, Ethan was on the top of the heap.

So was just about everyone he employed.

"I heard you scream. Are you okay?"

Mari liked the fact he didn't try and skirt around the fact she'd freaked out and woken him up, which was why she didn't bother denying the truth. "No, but I will be. Somehow, I will be."

"Good girl," he praised. He smiled, rose, and then held out his hand. "Come on, I know a couple tricks to the nightmare trade. I'll teach them to you."

He had nightmares?

She swallowed. Her gaze tracked to the large scar on his torso, dangerously near his heart. "What happened?"

"I dodged left and should have gone right," he replied. "Someone shot me while I was on a mission. I was captured, and then I was rescued. I don't remember much of the rescue, but I remember way too much about the in between."

The capture.

"I'm sorry," she whispered. "That must've been terrible.

"I survived. The rest of my team didn't," Ethan said. "It took me a lot of time to accept I had lived

93

even though they died. It took me even longer to learn how to cope with that so I could continue living in their honor."

Wow. Mari's eyes burned with emotion as she considered what he'd said. "I can't imagine what you endured."

"It's no worse than what you survived," he said.

"I doubt that," she whispered into the thickening silence.

"We survived. It doesn't matter which rung of hell we escaped. We escaped. Don't ever belittle what you went through, Mari. It's a part of you now. What you choose to shape it into will determine the type of person you are from this point forward." His jaw twitched as he ran a finger along the damaged side of her face. "I've seen firsthand what happens when a person only half survives what was done to them. In many ways, that's worse than death."

Her heart ached. "You knew someone who was abused. That's why you started Counterstrike."

"Counterstrike formed because of many things, but yes. That was one of them."

Who? The question seemed too invasive. He'd opened himself up enough already, offered her a big chunk of what'd shaped him after he escaped hell.

She'd take what he willingly gave and make the best of it, because he was right.

Chester hadn't ruined her. He'd tried, but she'd escaped his hell. Although he'd tried to punish her for leaving, she'd left. What she did from this point forward did shape her.

"Come on." He took her hand and headed out of the bedroom.

They went down the stairs and into the kitchen. He motioned toward a stool. She sat and watched as he pulled out ingredients from the pantry and a pot.

"My dad was an abusive dick. Mom took the brunt of it, but sometimes Milo or I would take our turns, mainly when we stepped between him and Mom." He pulled out a spoon and got to work putting cocoa and sugar into a pan. "He'd always storm out of the house after he'd meted out his hell. After we'd bandage what was hurt and clean up the mess, she'd always fix us cocoa. It's the first medicine in my arsenal."

Cocoa.

Her eyes burned with unshed tears as she imagined a little Ethan bruised. Battered. God.

"Is she…" She let the question trail off. Way, way too invasive.

He froze his movements. Intensity reflected in

his gaze when he looked at her. "She's alive. She's in a facility in Boerne, a private one Milo and I had formed with our trust accounts while we were in the service."

A facility. Mari's stomach churned. She forced the words poised on her tongue back, and waited through the silence as he continued making cocoa.

"She has Chronic Traumatic Encephalopathy, or CTE. It's happens with athletes, veterans, or anyone who sustains repetitive brain trauma. It didn't start appearing until a few years after she'd finally gotten away from him, just when her life was finally turning around." He turned, put the pot on the stove and turned it on. "That was several years ago. By the time Milo and I graduated high school, it'd progressed to early onset dementia. She made us promise we'd live the lives we wanted and not focus on her."

"Oh, God." Mari swallowed, unsure what else to say.

"Don't let him win. You three living life to its fullest despite him is a win for us all. Make him pay. That was her request to all three of us," Ethan said as he cleared his throat. "Milo is the public speaker of the family. He's spoken at many functions over the years, shared Mom's story. Ours. Sharing the story is testimony for her."

"Please tell me the bastard is dead," she said. She fisted her hands on the bar in front of her and held her breath as she waited for his answer.

"Blood thirsty," he said with a grin. "I like it."

"Is he?"

"No, but Milo and I ruined him. It took some doing, and too long for Mom to fully understand she'd finally well and truly won the war she'd fought for years. We didn't enter the final stage of our plans until we were out of the service. By then, the trust funds set up by our mother were turned over to us." He took Mari's hand. "She was wealthy, very much so. He was from an affluent family. The marriage was a societal one arranged by her parents, back when the rich did that sort of thing."

"That's horrible."

"Counterstrike is for her. We fight abusers, but we also fight social injustice. Anyone fighting a bigger dog in the yard deserves someone at their back. That's what we do."

"You're amazing," she whispered. "What you and Milo and Jen are doing is amazing."

"No." He shook his head and squeezed her hand. "What Mom did to get us away was amazing. All we're doing is following the lighted path she carved out. Counterstrike was her idea—one she shared long ago, over cups of hot cocoa. Back then, justice and freedom were illusive dreams, but we never stopped dreaming. Because she wouldn't let us."

"She's an amazing woman," Mari declared. One who'd escaped and gotten her three babies out. Safe.

Thank God I never had kids.

Mari suppressed the thought, ashamed that she'd had it just now. Mary felt as though she'd trampled on what his mom had survived by being grateful she'd never had children.

Chester had wanted to.

He'd tried forcing the issue many times. Fortunately there were lots of clinics with the three-month birth control shot. She'd gotten smart early on and kept the pills around as a smokescreen.

She cleared her throat as he gave her a cup of hot cocoa. She'd never been much of a fan, but suddenly nothing sounded better than a warm, steaming cup of sweet, chocolatey goodness in the dead of night. Especially one shared with a hot, sexy, kind, and considerate man.

CHAPTER 6

"What do you mean I can't go to work?" Mari stared at Ethan and Milo. They were crazy. "I have to work. Work pays my bills. Work keeps me sane. I need work."

Mari stared down at the uniform she'd salvaged from the pile of stuff Twitch and a couple other men she hadn't met yet had brought from her apartment. She was wrinkled and running at least a good fifteen minutes late, which meant she had zero time for this conversation.

"Look, I understand what you're saying, but I'm going to be in a public place. Trust me, at least five hundred people will be in and out of that coffee shop while I'm there. No one will be able to mess with me," she promised.

"It's not a good idea," Ethan said, his voice calm even though his eyes cut to his brother, as if silently asking for backup.

"He's right. Stay away at least one more day, then we'll figure out a protection detail."

"A protection detail?" She looked over at Jen, who sat at the small dining room table.

The woman glanced up. "Oh, right. Work. They're right, Mari. It's not a good idea to go to work yet, but they're also wrong. I understand you need the routine and normalcy work offers. And the money doesn't hurt either."

Mari crossed her arms and watched the brunette stand and get into position in front of her brothers.

"One man outside the shop just in case," Jen said.

"Two inside at all times," Ethan countered.

"Pfft." The brunette crossed her arms. "You know that won't fly. One inside."

The two men looked at one another. Milo shrugged.

"Fine, but I'm going."

"No, you aren't. You are both needed here and at the safehouses. Those Arsenal folks don't mess around."

"Twitch and Milo can handle them," Ethan said.

"I was up at five a.m. this morning with those women going over plans and details. Then I schlepped my ass around town rousing little kids and scared mommas out of their beds and out the door without breakfast in their bellies so our safehouses were emptied out. Do you know how many McDonalds I've been to today? Do you know how many eggs I've scrubbed off little faces?" Jen put a hand on her hip. "Too many, Ethan Evans Davenport. So you're on installations with Milo and Twitch and everyone else. Send Chatter."

"Chatter?" Milo asked, a smile on his face. "Why him?"

"Because he's *Chatter*," Jen shouted. "This conversation is over. She's going to work and Chatter will take her. We'll discuss her schedule for the rest of the week later, after we get those babies back in their beds and their mommas calmed down—something you two Casanovas are doing cause I'm up to my eyeballs in momma attitude and baby spittle. I handle legal briefs, not baby briefs."

"You mean diapers?" Ethan asked. "They're diapers, sis."

"Shut it. This conversation is over," Jen said. She looked over at Mari. "I'll text Chatter. He'll pick you up in a few minutes."

MARI UNDERSTOOD HOW CHATTER GOT HIS NICKNAME ten minutes into the ride to the coffee shop. He hadn't uttered a word. And he was huge. At least six foot six with thick, corded muscle.

Six hours into her supposed five-hour shift and he'd muttered a whopping ten words. She and Francine had a pool going with the two cooks on the grill. Mari had assumed he'd be forced into conversation at some point, but so far he'd maintained radio silence despite Francine's many, many attempts at dragging him into conversation.

Mari almost felt sorry for Chatter. He sat at the smallest, ricketiest table in the small eatery because it was the one closest to her at the register. His long torso was leaned back against the wall and although his eyes were shut, she suspected he was aware of every movement within the coffee house.

She'd survived another shift.

She breathed a sigh of relief when Francine latched the door closed and flipped the open sign over to display closed. The perky blonde trundled over on her four-inch wedges, grasped Mari's arm and squeezed.

"Okay, I was good and waited all shift to get

answers. Spill. What happened to your poor face?" The girl's blue eyes shimmered with unshed tears.

Mari had bypassed explanations when she'd arrived when Chatter's first gruff word boomed within the small coffee shop. *Later*. It'd been the only word necessary to get every employee far, far away from Mari.

She glanced over at Chatter, whose deep, black eyes penetrated her. The man was beyond intense. Hell, he likely snacked on intense for fun.

"Someone broke into my place," Mari said.

"Oh my God!" Francine touched Mari's face gently. "You poor thing. Do you need a place to stay? You can crash with me. That'd be fun. We could stay up all night and gab and I'll show you how to use makeup to cover your bruises. I learned all about that growing up cause my sister was always fighting."

Mari couldn't help but laugh. She'd never spent much time around the peppy, younger woman. She was working her way through part-time college classes "one java at a time" and had very little in common with Mari.

But she'd just offered her a place to stay.

"Thank you. That's very sweet, but I'm covered." She glanced over at Chatter.

"Oh. My. God. Is he your boyfriend?" The

woman shrieked the inquiry. Chatter chuckled and shifted in his seat. Arms crossed, he watched.

"No, he's a friend of a friend." Mari lowered her voice. "Come on, let's get to work on those dishes so we can get out of here. I don't know about you, but I'm ready to call it a day."

"I'd imagine so! You're likely exhausted from yesterday's ordeal."

Mari didn't offer comment. She was tired, but not nearly as tired as she'd been for months. Hell, years. Ethan had not only kept her head above the proverbial troubled waters, but he'd kept vigil at her side.

Cocoa.

She still tasted phantom dregs of the sweet concoction on her tongue, or she pretended to at least. They'd sat on the sofa in the living room and chatted about nonsensical stuff until her mind moved beyond the break-in, past the attack, and invested fully in getting to know Ethan.

Mari got to work scrubbing pots and pans left-over from the late evening dinner crowd. Even though they primarily sold coffee, they also offered a limited menu of grilled items.

"There you are." Cindy's voice punctured Mari's happy bubble.

To say Cindy was a spiteful bitch of a boss was an

understatement. Mari swiped her hand on her sweaty brow and stood fully. Soapy water dripped from both her hands.

"The police were here earlier today asking questions about you."

Oh God.

"Did you get arrested?" Cindy asked.

"No. I told you, someone broke into my apartment and attacked me last night."

"Then why were they here asking about you?" Cindy demanded.

"I'm not sure. Maybe you should ask them."

"I've had enough of your attitude, Marisol. I've been more than patient with you," Cindy said. Arms crossed, she glowered. "Punch out, go sit in the employee lounge, and wait for me. The police are on their way."

"What?" Fear crawled up her throat.

"What's wrong?" Francine asked as she exited the walk-in fridge.

"Get Chatter."

"Don't you dare," Cindy warned. "That man has no business in this place, much less back here."

"Get Chatter," Mari repeated. "Cindy, I have to go."

"You aren't going anywhere. I called them before

we closed. They're likely almost here. Whatever you did, you aren't getting away with it."

No. No. No. No. No.

She'd told Ethan she'd be safe here because Chester and his minion friends had never, ever bothered her at work. It was an invisible line she'd started to take for granted. As long as she was at work, she was safe.

But she wasn't tonight thanks to Cindy.

"You don't understand. My ex-husband is a cop. An abusive asshole."

"I don't care if he's the King of England. You're coming with me, punching out, and waiting for the cops." Cindy grabbed Mari's upper arm and jerked. Hard.

Pain ran up her arm and along her shoulder. She moved to push the woman off, but Cindy was gone.

Chatter stood in front of her glaring at the woman sprawled on the floor.

"Wow. That. Was. Hot." Francine's declaration knocked a bit of the shock from Mari's system. What the heck had just happened?

"Car."

The single word was all the order Mari needed. He was right. They needed to get to the car and get the heck away before the cops came. She didn't need

Chatter getting arrested for assaulting her boss and whatever cops who arrived. Mari had no doubt he'd lay them all out if they moved to mess with her.

She yanked off her apron, grabbed her purse, and moved toward the employee entrance to the café. Blue and red lights swirled. Two police cruisers parked behind the three cars parked in the rear lot.

Blocked in.

Adrenaline spiked within her.

Her pulse thundered in her ears.

"Stay behind me," Chatter ordered.

Mari obeyed. Her knees knocked against one another as two uniformed officers came from the left and another two arrived from the right. Two hovered their hands near their belt as all their gazes remained on Chatter.

"Sir, step away from the woman with your hands locked behind your head," one of them ordered.

"She's under my protection."

"Sir, step away from the woman with your hands locked behind your head," the officer repeated.

"Just do it," Mari pleaded. She didn't want Chatter riddled with bullets. "Call Ethan. And Jen."

"Marisol Santos is under Counterstrike protection. Her attorney is in route. Any move to take her into custody without cause will be deemed a physical threat to her person—one I *will* react to accordingly." Chatter's voice was steely as he stood his ground, hands fisted at his sides. "I will step aside and allow you to proceed once her attorney is present and you have demonstrated probable cause to be here. Or a warrant."

"We cannot discuss an ongoing investigation," one of the officers said.

"Investigation? About her break-in?" Francine asked, her phone up. "I'm recording this, by the way. Her crazy ex isn't messing with her anymore. Nuh uh."

"Ms. Santos, you need to come with us," one of the officers said. "Tell them to stand down or we'll be forced to take them all into custody."

"Please try," Chatter said, a leery smirk on his face as he turned to look at Mari.

Of all the times for Chatter to start talking, why did it have to be now? Goading the police didn't seem like a smart move, but she had to admit it gave them pause. They looked at one another warily, as if trying to figure out how to proceed.

"Call it in," one of them ordered.

One of them stepped away. The one who'd issued the order moved forward and motioned for the other two to stand down.

"I'm Officer Hampton. We're within our rights to take Ms. Santos in as ordered, but we will wait as you requested. I'm fully aware of Counterstrike and what you do. If she's under your protection, there's more going on than we were told."

Chatter grunted, interlocking his hands behind his body. Mari took another step forward until she was fully at his side.

"Behind me," Chatter growled.

"You aren't getting riddled with bullets because of me," Mari said.

Officer Hampton's gaze narrowed when his gaze moved to her. She suspected he hadn't seen her face yet. None of them had since she'd been hiding behind Chatter.

"Someone broke into my place last night and attacked me. Is that why you're here?"

"No, ma'am. We were asked to bring you in for questioning by the Homicide Division."

Homicide? Shock rolled through her system, followed quickly by anger. Chester was in Homicide. He had a hell of a lot of nerve dragging her in.

"Who the hell did I supposedly murder?"

"Ma'am, we do not know anything beyond the fact we were asked to bring you in for questioning," Officer Hampton said.

"Thank God you all are here. Arrest this man," Cindy ordered as she shoved her way around Chatter. "He attacked me."

"Sir, did you assault this woman?" Officer Hampton asked with a sigh.

"Yes."

Shock rippled through the assembled officers. They regarded one another.

"She touched my charge without permission. I responded after she caused her physical harm," Chatter said with a shrug. "I may have responded with more force than necessary, but no one harms a woman around me without feeling the consequences."

"I did not assault her, and I certainly did not harm her," Cindy spat angrily. "He's lying."

"You grabbed her arm," Francine said. "I saw it my own damn self. And you yanked her. Hard."

"Is that true?" Officer Hampton asked.

"Yes," Mari said. "I bruise easily. You can probably see her hand print bruising my arm soon enough." If it weren't for the other ones already there. She forced the thought aside and looked at the officer. "I'd really, really like to go home, sir. Please. I promise I'll go to the station with my attorney first thing in the morning. I'm tired, my body hurts, and I can't deal with anything else today.

"I'm afraid letting you leave isn't an option, ma'am, but we'll wait for your attorney."

"Ma'am, is one of these men the one who assaulted you last night?"

Mari blinked and rubbed her eyes as Detective Higgs set a piece of paper with six pictures in front of her. Although exhaustion blurred her eyes slightly, it took less than two seconds for her to spot the bastard. The center bottom one.

But he looked...

Her stomach pitched. Words formed on the edge of her tongue, but she didn't let them out. Instead, she reached over and squeezed Ethan's hand. Terror crawled up her throat.

"What's wrong?" He leaned in. "If you don't recognize him, that's okay. We'll find him either way. I promised you he'd pay."

Oh God. No. No. No. No. No.

Whatever sick game Chester had been playing with her had just entered the next level of hell. She swallowed and forced the words out. "I need a moment alone with my attorney."

Jen tensed beside her. "You heard my client."

"That's not an option until I get an answer to my question," Higgs replied.

Mari looked at Jen, who nodded. "Center bottom."

"There's your answer," Jen said. "A moment. Now."

Detective Higgs scraped his chair along the concrete floor. His lip curled up at the edge as he grabbed the pictures and looked around the room. "Three minutes."

"Five, or however long we need, Detective." Jen glared and waited for the man to leave. The moment he did, she looked at Mari. "What's wrong?"

"He's dead."

"I'm sorry, what?"

"The guy who..." She swallowed. "He's dead. Why else would a homicide detective be asking me about my assault? Think about it. Evidence was found on scene to tie that guy to Chester, right? Or someone hiring him to hurt me."

"He tied up loose ends," Ethan said. "Which means you're in even more danger than before, because you're the biggest loose end of all."

"What do I do?" Mari asked, not caring which of them answered. She'd do whatever either of them said because she was terrified. Absolutely, certifiably terrified.

Ethan pointed at the small pin on the collar of his shirt. "The little cam Zoey gave us snapped the image. She and Tex are working together to get info right now. Hold tight."

"How do you know that?" Mari asked.

Ethan pointed at his ear. Relief filled her. Of course. He'd come ready for war with a team behind his back.

No. Two teams, three if they counted Tex. Mari figured he was a team all on his own.

"Hang tight. We'll have information coming at us soon enough. Milo, get Nitro on the streets. We need answers stat." Ethan squeezed her hand. "They can't pin that on you, Mari. You've been with us every second since I arrived on scene."

"He's not going after me," she whispered, giving voice to her newest fear. "He's going after you. Counterstrike. You're his target, not me."

CHAPTER 7

"FUCK, SHE'S RIGHT, BRO. IT MAKES SENSE," MILO said in Ethan's ear. "You'd best get out while you can."

"That's not an option," he declared. No way in hell was Ethan going to leave Mari and Jen there with the sharks. "We've got him running scared, which means there's more to find. We missed something."

"He's right." The calm, female voice on the other end of the com startled him a moment. It wasn't upbeat and high like Zoey. Silky, deep and almost... seductive. "Quillery and I are tagging in, Z. We'll coordinate with Tex, but we've brought Hera online."

"Who's Hera?" Milo asked.

"Not a who, a what. H-E-R-A. An acronym. HERA. That's the system they designed. Think big brother with a brain and badass gadgets," Zoey said. "It can do just about anything in a nanosecond."

Ethan didn't give a damn if they resurrected the goddess Hera herself as long as they got some freaking answers. He shifted restlessly in is chair as Detective Higgins entered the room.

"Don't say anything," Jen advised. "I'll handle it from here. They aren't messing with either of you, or anyone else."

"We're bringing Tex onto the com," another female voice said. "He's got full access to HERA. Z, we need you online to help Cord and Jacob close our gaps."

"Objective?" Zoey asked.

"Data. We're pulling all security footage we can get our hands on for the past seventy-two hours. South and East Austin."

"Okay, Quillery. Which areas?" Zoey asked.

"I just told you. South and East Austin."

"All of South and East Austin," Edge clarified. "If it's a camera and it recorded something, we're taking the footage."

"And then?" Tex asked.

"Then we tag HERA in," Quillery said. "Ckay,

good news is there were government drones flying overhead. The bad news is there were government drones flying overhead. This'll take time, less than normal with Tex helping, but it'll take time."

"I've got someone else we can pull in," Tex offered.

"We're good," Edge said. "Three of us, three on our backs handling security and cleaning our trail. Anymore and it could get dicey."

"I'm ready when you are," Tex said. "Keep them chasing their tail, Gemini."

Ethan smiled as the detective sat down. He shoved the picture back in front of Mari, who recoiled like it was a rattlesnake. A growl rose from Ethan's throat.

"Where were you yesterday evening, around nine?" Detective Higgins asked.

"Hank's," Jen said, smoothly and silkily. She leaned back in her chair. "I believe there was a verbal altercation between my client and an officer occurring at the time."

"Roger Westerman," Mari supplied. "We were discussing my grievous inability to be a good wife and take the beatings my ex-husband, Detective Chester Rollins, gave me during our marriage for the slightest infractions, such as being unable to read his mind. And not accepting his decision to cheat. I'm sure there was more we discussed, but that's what I recall."

Ethan chuckled. Jen glowered at him.

"I'll need a full list of your personnel, Mr. Davenport."

"On what grounds?" Jen asked.

"Your organization is gathering a reputation, Ms. Davenport. One where everyone knows Counterstrike will do anything and everything needed to keep its clients safe."

"And you think that includes murder," Ethan said.

"Does it?"

Ethan shrugged. "A man hurts a woman, he deserves whatever justice gets meted."

"Shut it," Jen whisper-shouted.

The detective smiled smugly. "You and your brother have quite the service record. It's a shame you mucked all that up by opening up Counterstrike and hiring mercenaries to work for you. Do you even bother running background checks on your employees any longer? I understand you have more than one convicted felon working for you."

"That's right," Ethan said, a measure of pride in his voice. "I'd crawl through the bowels of hell for both of them, and everyone on my team for that matter. Can you say the same about those you work with, Detective? Do you think Detective Rollins would do that for you?"

"This isn't about Detective Rollins," the man said.

"And here I thought you had a brain of your own to use," Ethan said.

"What part of I'll handle this did you not understand?" Jen asked.

"This is rather simple. Turn over your employee roster, and we'll go from there," the man said.

"That's not happening without a warrant."

"Easy enough," the man said smugly.

"A federal one," Edge said in Ethan's ear.

"Come again," he said.

"HERA is classified. It's considered a potential threat to national security if it falls into the wrong hands. A federal warrant will be needed to touch any and all Counterstrike assets and locations as long as the systems we just installed are in place. One flip of the switch and you have full access to an intelligence system every alphabet agency in the world is trying to get," Quillery said. "Some local yokel with his hands down his jammies isn't authorized to mess with you."

Holy shit.

Tex whistled. "Well, I didn't see that one coming."

Ethan couldn't help but chuckle.

"Don't worry, I called Bob. He's gonna sort the whole not-authorized-for-a-warrant thing," Quillery said.

"Bob?" Milo asked.

"Don't ask. You don't want to know," Zoey replied. "Just roll with it, Gemini. It's the only way to survive the Quillery Edge."

Ethan hadn't seen the price tag for the security system they'd installed, but it had just paid for itself ten times over. Yet another debt owed to Nolan Mason.

And Tex.

"I guess we're done talking until you get that warrant, Detective." A warrant he was definitely not getting anytime soon if what Edge and Quillery said was true.

"I'll be back soon. You may as well go ahead and make the list," the man suggested as he rose. "We've got more than one judge on speed dial."

"I'm sure you do," Ethan said, his tone as mocking and condescending as he could make it.

"Enough," Jen growled when the man left. "What the hell has gotten into you?"

"You'll see soon enough," he said, taking a certain amount of amusement in being one-up on Jen about anything legal for the first time in...well, forever. He wrapped an arm around Mari and whispered, "It's going to be okay. They can't touch us."

"I hope you're right."

"Tex, Zoey, and everyone else is working on getting data right now. Nitro's already hitting the streets to gather information. No one gets answers easier than him, not even Tex. Whatever happened, we'll know soon enough. Until then, you aren't alone. We aren't going anywhere. None of us are."

"Thank you."

"Don't ever thank me for doing what everyone should have done a long time ago, Mari. Your ex never should've gotten the chance to mess with you just because he's a cop. He may be the law, but that doesn't make him above it."

Mari had been through enough.

"Internal Affairs and the Texas Rangers have been apprised of current events," Milo said.

Thank fuck. Ethan didn't give a damn who took Chester and his cronies down as long as they went down. Hard. He'd been on teams too long to give a damn about being the one to do the deed. The end result was all that mattered.

Which was why Ethan leaned back in his chair, crossed his arms, and waited when the detective returned to the room.

"Let's start from the beginning, shall we?" Detective Higgins asked. "Who are your employees and where were they at nine the evening in question?"

Ethan grinned.

"The sooner you cooperate, the better. I realize Ms. Santos is not responsible for what happened. Give me what I need and she can leave."

Right. Like Ethan would let her leave the station without protection. He deepened the grin and hoped to hell the magical Bob—whoever the fuck he was—had the clout Quillery thought he did. Otherwise it was going to be a very long, boring night for them all.

It didn't matter either way, though, because as long as the detective was focused on getting answers from Ethan, everyone else could keep digging and get the answers they needed to once and for all put a nail on Chester's coffin.

It looked like they'd be taking a lot more people than just Chester down, though. There had to have been quite a few people involved to manipulate the situation enough to implicate Counterstrike in anything, especially a murder. Sure, they hadn't outright accused anyone of anything.

They hadn't even admitted the asshole who'd hurt Mari was dead.

"Jessica just confirmed he's in the county morgue awaiting autopsy," Milo said. "He was a low-level runner for the SouthSiders. Nitro's working his contacts to get intel."

A small part of Ethan wanted to order Nitro back, make him lie low until the dust cleared. But standing between the bad guys and the people Counterstrike protected was what they'd all signed on to do. He couldn't order anyone back, not when they were just as invested in the situation as he was.

He looked over at the beautiful woman next to him and sighed. No one was as invested as Ethan when it came to Mari. There was no denying he was attracted to her. She was his to protect and care for. Call it mancave Alpha dog assholedness, or whatever. Ethan didn't give a damn.

Mari was his. He'd give her as much time as she needed to come to the same decision, to accept what he already knew. He was a patient man.

"This isn't a game, Mr. Davenport. I will get the

answers I want, one way or another. The only person's time you're wasting here is Marisol's."

Ethan leaned forward and settled his elbows on the table. He cleared his throat to speak but caught a flash of suits moving briskly through the corridors leading to the room they'd been escorted into. He chuckled, leaned back in his seat, and crossed his arms again.

"Let the games begin," he replied.

"Detective Higgins, I'm Agent Racquards from Homeland Security. This is Mr. Whit from the Department of Defense. We understand you wish to obtain a search warrant for Counterstrike facilities."

"That's right," Detective Higgins said as he shuffled in his seat. "I'm sorry, but this is a closed investigation. You'll have to follow the proper chain of command if you wish to assist our investigation."

Mari choked as the tension within the room struck a new level of weird. Ethan was outright smiling for some reason she couldn't comprehend. Jen was in full-blown shock and neither of the men in the suits were very pleased with the situation.

"I'm afraid you misunderstand our presence,

Detective. Your investigation is done." Mr. Whit looked at Mari, then at Ethan and Jen. "You three are free to leave with our apologies. I've been instructed to handle Detective Higgins from here and redirect his investigation away from matters of national security."

"National security?" Detective Higgins sputtered the words as he rose and stood in front of the exit. "They're a nonprofit helping a bunch of women and kids. How is that national security?"

"What Counterstrike is or isn't in the eyes of Homeland Security and the Department of Defense is above your paygrade, Detective," Agent Racquards said. "Kindly step away from the door so Ms. Santos and the Davenports may leave."

"This is ridiculous. I demand to see your credentials immediately. This is not proper protocol."

"Neither is obtaining search warrants on national security assets without proper authority," Mr. Whit replied. "We're done here. Please feel free to leave at any time, Ms. Santos, with our deepest apologies. You won't be bothered about Samual Rivers' murder again."

Samual Rivers. Her nightmare had a name. She nodded and let Ethan steer her from the room. She didn't pretend to understand what'd just happened.

Jen's high heels tapped a comforting click-clack rhythm along the tiled corridor leading to the exit.

Each step helped Mari breath a bit more.

They were leaving. Truly leaving.

But how?

"Just keep walking, one foot in front of the other," Ethan whispered in her ear.

Cool air rushed across her face when they exited the building. She dragged in deep breaths despite her broken ribs. To hell with the pain. She'd gotten out. Sure, she realized on some higher level she wasn't ever in any true danger of being arrested just now.

But Ethan was.

Or whoever at Counterstrike they could hit.

All because Chester was making a point.

All because of her.

"I've gotta go," she declared. "This isn't safe for you, or for your team, or anyone. I've gotta go. Leave town, the country, or something. I don't even have a passport. But I've gotta go. I've gotta disappear."

"Take a deep breath for me. It's okay."

"No. No, it's not okay. None of what just happened is okay. I don't even know what just happened."

"Neither do I, Mari, but we'll talk it out once

we're away from here and we have you secure," Jen said, her voice firm. "Let's go."

Let's go. The woman made it sound so simple. Maybe it was in a way. But going never lasted. Getting secure only worked for so long. Then Chester would continue meting out his punishment.

All because she'd wanted a husband who loved her, one who truly cared about her. One who'd hold her close, kiss away her tears when she'd had a bad day and kick anyone's ass if they messed with her. She'd wanted a man who was strong, brilliant, thoughtful, and protective.

Like Ethan.

The thought shuffled through her brain until it found a place to settle down.

And it did because he was a great man, one she couldn't deny being attracted to.

The thought flickered through her mind like a butterfly fluttering about for no other reason than to chase away the scary situation sucking the breath from her lungs. Ethan was here. His arms were around her.

He was whispering words she couldn't hear because she was freaking out, but she wasn't alone. She dragged in another breath and battled her way through the fear.

For Ethan.

He'd put his ass on the line for her.

She wouldn't turn wuss on him outside the police department.

But she needed him to understand why her staying around and letting them help her was no longer an option. She didn't fully know what had happened just now, but they'd dodged a huge bullet —one aimed directly at Counterstrike.

They were too important to get hurt because of her. The work they did changed lives and saved people. She could endure Chester's games. Sooner or later he'd find another woman and move on.

The thought doused her with guilt. She couldn't let anyone else suffer what she'd gone through. No. No one else should have to deal with Chester.

He needed to be stopped.

Which meant she needed to stay and trust that Ethan and everyone else at Counterstrike knew what the hell they were doing.

God, she wished Joseph was there to give her big brotherly wisdom. He always knew what to say. And her parents.

Mari would do just about anything to have her parents hug her, hold her close. Her mom's chocolate chip cookies would make her feel better.

"What's going through your mind? Offload it, Mari. You aren't alone."

"I was just wishing my brother was here to give me some advice. I'm terrified, Ethan. I want to run because I don't want you or anyone at Counterstrike hurt by him and all this, but I know if I get away he'll put someone else through this. And that's not fair." She spewed the truth out so fast the words jumbled together in the end. "AndImissmymom'schocolate-chipcookies."

Before she could second guess the decision, she wrapped her arms around Ethan, rested her head on his chest, and let the tears fall. To hell with being strong.

"Ethan," Jen whispered.

"Get the car. I've got her," he instructed. "It's okay, Mari. I've got you. It's going to be okay. I swear to Christ I'll make it all okay."

CHAPTER 8

Warmth and pleasure drifted within her. The aches and discomfort she'd tried to ignore ceded to a cascade of feminine awareness. She sighed in contentment and let the sensations carry her away. She drifted on a cloud...

A hard, muscular, and hot cloud.

Mari blinked awake and inhaled the oaky musk she recognized as Ethan's distinctive scent. She relished the smell of him permeating her nostrils as her gaze swept up the hard ridges of his chest.

"You're awake." His entire body rumbled beneath her, but his voice was soft, quiet.

Deft fingers ran through her hair to graze her scalp in a gentle massage. Awareness beaded along her skin as the touch firmed along the base on her neck and moved in a distinctive pattern.

M. Oh God. She squeezed her eyes closed and savored the contact, the slow sweep of his touch.

A. The top of the letter formed at the base of her scalp. She trembled from the contact there. How long had it been since she'd felt a lover's touch? Had a man want her, not as a possession, but a woman?

R. The sweep around to form the top of the letter became a slow, almost seductive glide along the back of her neck. She opened her eyes, peering into Ethan's. He'd be an excellent lover, the kind who was attentive and patient. Who'd make sure she enjoyed it just as much as he did.

I. She tracked the movement of his Adam's apple as he swallowed. She traced her finger there and slowly spelled out her request.

Breath held, she formed the first letter along the span of his throat. They were on a bed she didn't recognize, so she assumed it was his. She didn't bother looking around. Instead, she kept her gaze locked on his as she formed the first letter.

K. His eyebrows furrowed, but he made no comment, as if not wanting to sever the tentative bond forming between them.

I. His grip in her hair firmed. Her nipples hardened as a flare of arousal pooled between her legs. God, it'd been so long since a man grasped her hair like that. Like he was about to hold her in place to lay claim and take whatever he wanted. And give in return.

S. A low rumble ran through him as she splayed a palm on his chest. She silently cursed the thin material of his T-shirt. She held her breath as she returned her finger to where it'd begun to form the final letter. Her request.

S. The compulsion to taste him was too much as she closed the scant distance between them until their lips feathered across one another. The contact was so soft, if she hadn't watched she would've thought she'd imagined it.

His grip remained, but he made no move to sever the contact, or deepen it. She'd never taken the lead with a man. Chester had been her first and only, which was a shamefully embarrassing thing to admit since he'd sucked in bed.

You're a lousy lay. Jesus, I should whore you out on the corner just so you could learn what to do with your mouth. You're pathetic.

The grip in her hair firmed until she opened her eyes. She hadn't realized she'd squeezed them shut.

"Mari," he said.

"Please," she pled, hoping he knew what she needed. Because at that point she wasn't even sure herself. All she knew was that for the first time since she could remember, she felt like a woman.

A beautiful, passionate woman capable of enjoying the touch of a man like Ethan Davenport. A real man.

But what if she did suck in bed? God, that would be so humiliating.

No, it wouldn't because Ethan was a kind, compassionate, and wonderful man. He'd make it okay, even if she sucked in bed. He'd never tell her. Somehow she knew that wasn't his style.

"Don't," he whispered against her lips.

"Don't what?"

"Don't let the bastard steal another second of you, Mari," he ordered. "Your new life starts here, this second. Right here. Promise me."

"Yes," she muttered, trailing the tip of her tongue along his bottom lip. "I'll promise for a kiss."

He growled as he firmed the contact. Awareness ignited along her skin and burrowed into her as he deepened the kiss. She surrendered to his tongue, gave chase and nipped when he nibbled. The languid, heated fusion stoked embers of need left dormant far too long.

One hand in her hair and the other holding her chin, he taunted her mouth, promising sensual delights her entire body responded to. He plunged, sucked, bit, licked, and teased. Her mouth was his playground in a way she'd never experienced.

Slow, methodical.

Playful.

Commanding.

She'd always thought kissing was disgusting. Repulsive.

Not with Ethan.

A moan escaped her as need spiraled within her. Her nipples hardened to achy nubs. She writhed against his side, but the contact wasn't enough. She wrapped her legs around his thigh and squeezed until he thrust it up until it rested against her achy core.

God, yes.

Words wouldn't form. They clung in her throat, but she feared speaking. The hazy fog of sensual bliss they were enveloped in was unlike anything she'd ever experienced.

She was desperate to not screw up.

She ground down on his thigh and groaned into his mouth. Her hand wandered beneath his T-shirt. Muscles bunched and flexed beneath her touch.

"Ethan, please." She whispered the words against his throat when he severed their kiss. He nibbled her earlobe as she rocked against his thigh once more. She was so, so close.

"Jesus, sweetheart, you're killing me," he whispered.

"I need you," she pled. "Please."

"Look at me, Mari," he demanded as the grip in her hair returned.

"Don't stop, please."

"Walking across an ocean would be easier than doing the right thing and stopping," he said. He kissed her lips gently. Eyes open, she peered into his and relished the glide of his mouth across hers.

It was the most intimate thing she'd ever experienced. Looking into his eyes from so close, she could swear she saw straight into his soul.

"But I'm stopping this now because you aren't ready. *We* aren't ready," he said. "Whatever this is between us is too important to rush. You are too important to rush."

"But..." She halted her argument when he placed his thumb across her lips. She sucked it into her mouth.

Arousal flared within her when his eyes widened as she sucked his thumb. She'd never been so bold and demanding with Chester. Ethan was different, though. She felt...

Safe.

Like he'd make whatever happened between them okay.

Because she mattered.

Enough to not rush into sex.

"Jesus, Mari. You have no idea how much I want you."

The prominent bulge against her gave her an idea, but he was right. It was too soon. She nestled back against him and drifted within the arousal he'd ignited within her.

She wasn't broken after all. She'd once thought she was. Chester always said it was her fault, not his.

But she'd promised not to give Chester another second of herself. Somehow doing so while in a bed curled against Ethan felt...wrong. Her bastard ex didn't have any place in her life, most especially in her bed.

"Where are we?" She looked up at him.

"My room. I was going to take you into the guest room, but you were so out of it when I carried you in, I wanted you in my bed where I could watch you while you slept, in case you had another nightmare."

"No one's ever worried about me like that before, except for my brother and parents."

"Then you're overdue," he declared. "Don't go anywhere. I'm going to go fix you some cocoa."

"Okay." She sighed when he left the bed, which felt much colder without him in it.

Without him curled against her.

She burrowed into the sheets and inhaled his scent. For tonight, she'd pretend she didn't have crazy a psycho ex-husband making her life a living hell. For now she was just a woman enjoying a gorgeous, sexy as hell man who kissed like a god.

COCOA. IT'D BEEN THE CRAZIEST EXCUSE TO GET OUT of the bed, but Ethan had taken it because he was one sigh and half a moan away from saying to hell with doing the right thing. A man could only take so much, and a sexy, responsive as hell Mari was too much to resist.

He froze as voices from inside the kitchen drifted into the hall.

"Well how the ever loving tarnation do I do that?" Zoey asked.

"How would I know?" Edge asked.

"You don't cook?" Zoey asked.

"Does ramen count?"

"Fine. Vi, what am I doing wrong?"

Edge laughed. "You think she's any better at cooking than I am?"

"Seriously? You are two brilliant women, the fiercest back office operatives in existence. You've led entire armies into battle, and you've never failed on a mission," Zoey said, then paused. "And neither one of you can cook?"

"Nope," Quillery said.

Ethan smiled and leaned against the open entryway to the kitchen. Milo sidled up and leaned against the other side. The three women had their heads pressed together and were peering into a bowl of what he assumed was flour, since almost an entire bag of the white substance coated their granite countertops.

His smile deepened as he looked at his OCD twin. To say he was a master chef was an understatement. He'd inherited their mom's passion for cooking more out of necessity than desire at first. Back when they'd first escaped their father, she'd been in good enough shape to cook and tend to them.

Within a couple years, though, the simplest task

of fixing eggs proved disastrous. Ethan shoved the unwanted memory away and focused on the three women. It was damn near three in the morning.

"I know. I'll call Ellie. She can bake anything," Zoey declared.

"Don't you dare call her," Edge ordered. "She's asleep."

"So?"

"She's not an operative, Z. She's the Office Manager. We don't get to call her at three in the morning because we can't bake chocolate chip cookies."

"This is nuts. Tex put us in charge of getting the parents. Big freaking whoop." Zoey sighed long and loud, then peered into the bowl. "We've fought drug cartels, found two kids in millions of acres of woods, taken down the biggest, nastiest black ops groups in existence, and we can't make a dozen cookies."

"Only a dozen?" Edge rubbed her belly. "I was thinking three, maybe four dozen."

Ethan smiled. She was pregnant. The barbecue and get-to-know-each-other end to the exhaustive day had been tabled for another time, but he'd put enough pieces together throughout the day before the police showed up at Mari's work place.

She and Vi were married.

Edge and Quillery. The Quillery Edge.

Their system had kept the locals off their asses and would ensure Mari and all the others Counter-strike protected were safe. He looked at his brother, motioning toward the disaster the women had made of their kitchen.

But a phone was ringing.

"Hello?"

"Ellie?"

"Yeah?" The voice was mumbled and confused, from what Ethan assumed was sleep.

"We have a critical mission we need your help with. I think we have everything we need, but how do we make chocolate chip cookies?" Zoey studied the crap splayed around her like she was about to declare war. "We need slow, clear, and concise instructions. We're making these for a woman whose been through hell, got out, then got dragged right back in. She's missing her mom and her cookies. This is on you, chica."

Damn.

This was for Mari.

He wasn't a master chef like his brother, but he was passable. He could sure as hell follow instructions online for cookie making. How hard could it be?

"Jesus," Milo muttered. "Let's go in before they blow up the oven. How is she?"

"Strong as hell, determined. Exhausted." He sighed. "Amazing."

"You're in deep quick."

"Yeah, but I'm not rushing her or us. We've got time after we get her through this mess."

"She's worth waiting for," Milo said.

"Yeah, she is. Let's get in there before they declare war on our kitchen. I heard they've never failed on a mission. Cookies for Mari can't be their first failure," Ethan teased.

The women turned as a unit when he and Milo entered the fray. Flour was everywhere. The women's faces, the floor. The ceiling.

"How did..." Milo bit off the question as he peered up at the vaulted ceiling.

"I tried to sift the flour with the blender. That didn't go too well," Zoey admitted.

"You don't need to sift flour for cookies," Ellie said. "I'm forcing you three into a cooking class when you get back."

"No, you aren't," Vi said.

"Yeah, I am. Addy and Kamren will make you come."

"Sorry they woke you, Ellie. We'll take it from here," Ethan said as he pushed the end call button and set the phone as far away from the flour zone as possible.

"What the hell did you do that for? Now she won't answer when I call her back. She's the best baker I know. She makes homemade jellies in little jars and shit like that. She could talk us through cookies while in a coma."

"These are for Mari?" Ethan asked, already knowing the answer.

"Yeah," Zoey said. "Mostly. Mary's eating for two, so the little peanut needs at least a dozen."

Milo chuckled.

"Dylan told you to stop calling our baby a peanut," Mary said.

"Well he's not here and I think it's adorable. And it's not like I can call Vi's little Jud a peanut when she starts baking him 'cause I'm not calling Jud's kid anything cute. Or little. He still scares me," Zoey admitted.

"He's harmless," Vi said.

"Can we please move past talking about the baby and get the cookies made? I'm hungry."

"More like hangry," Zoey muttered. "Okay, fine. You two think you know what the hell you're doing? Prove it. Let Operation Cookie Dough commence."

Ethan chuckled and looked at his brother. "Guess we're officially tagged in."

CHAPTER 9

Cookies were everywhere. Mari tentatively followed a wary June Bug into the kitchen and looked around at the piles and piles of cookies. Sugary goodness hung in the air. A faint white cloud drifted within the rays of the sun coming in from the window along the back wall. Was that flour?

She looked up at the ceiling and smiled. A film of white coated the vaulted ceiling. She tiptoed past the women passed out atop one another much like a pile of puppies. Suitcases sat near the garage entryway, which Mari found strange. She supposed they'd brought the supplies in them.

She snatched a chocolate chip cookie from the massive mound and took a big bite. It wouldn't be as good as Mom's, but it'd do. Hopefully they wouldn't mind that she'd taken one. Shock rolled through her as she chewed.

Mom's secret ingredients.

Cinnamon. Mint.

How did they know?

"Marisol."

Mari spun as shock turned to outright joy. She screamed and ran toward her mom and dad. They grunted with the force of impact but squeezed her tight. Her damaged ribs hurt, but the grip eased quickly enough for her to breathe. Tears streamed down her face as her mom and dad kissed her and whispered consoling words at her in a mix of English and Spanish.

"You should have called us sooner," her mom admonished as she pulled away.

Mari had inherited her mom's short stature. The woman stood at four foot eleven, but swore she'd once been five foot two. Tears pooled in her mom's eyes.

And Dad.

His face was a mixture of hurt, shock, rage, and relief. She hugged him tighter. "I'm okay, Papa."

"No, you aren't. But you will be."

"How did you get here?"

"A very nice woman phoned us and told us what

all was happening," her mom said. "Never again, *hija*. Never again do you keep something like this from us."

"It's not ever happening again, Mrs. Santos," Ethan said as he entered the kitchen.

"Ah, yes, you have told us so, and I believe you." Her mom smiled and patted Ethan's cheek. "Come, I fix breakfast. Cookies can wait."

Mari wiped away the tears of joy and looked up at Ethan. "You knew about this?"

"Yeah. The Arsenal women are responsible for most of this, including the mounds of cookies."

"Erm, no. We're responsible for the disaster zone your kitchen was *before* you and your brother came down and rescued Operation Cookie Dough," Zoey corrected as she lifted June Bug and gave her belly scratches. "Then your mom arrived and showed us how to add her secret ingredients."

Mari smiled. Momma had a special skill for cooking, one Mari wished she'd inherited. Operation Cookie Dough. She glanced about the room, over to the three exhausted women on the floor. They'd been making cookies. Why?

"We wanted to surprise you," the brunette said. "I'm Mary, by the way. This is Vi. I don't think we've met yet. You were pretty out of it last night. Did you sleep okay?"

Mari blinked and nodded as Ethan touched her back. "They're with The Arsenal. They're helping Tex with the electronic surveillance investigation into the murder."

"Right. The murder."

She'd somehow almost forgotten that someone had murdered the man who'd broken into her home and hurt her. She looked over at her parents and noted the way her father cocooned her mom along his side, much like Ethan had her just now. Mari leaned into Ethan's powerful frame.

Despite the harrowing ordeal they were all enduring, the moment was almost perfect. The only person missing was Joseph. Mari needed to send him an email. No matter where he was, or how busy he might be, he always tried to check his email whenever he could. He'd infrequently be able to Skype, or he'd pop into messenger and surprise her.

But Tex had mentioned he was on a mission, which meant he likely couldn't do any of that anytime soon. She hoped he was okay and being careful.

"I'll help fix breakfast, Mrs. Santos," Milo offered.

"Bueno, bueno. You are a good boy and a good cook. You chop potatoes and onions. I'll do the rest." The woman shuffled into the kitchen and donned an apron hanging from the stove, the exact place Mom hung hers in her kitchen.

Mari couldn't help but smile. Mom had already taken over the kitchen like it was hers. She flashed a grateful smile to Milo when he fell into step alongside her mom without comment or argument. He smirked as he started chopping potatoes and onions.

"If she gets out of control, let me know and I'll try to rein her in," Mari whispered to Ethan.

"She's fine. It's nice to have a mom in the house, to be honest. It's been a while." Pain glinted in his gaze when he looked down at her. "She and I came to an understanding earlier when she tried to go upstairs and wake you. She understands my boundaries, and so does your dad. We're good."

She understood his boundaries and so did her dad? Questions fell into line in her brain, but she didn't give them voice. Her heart swelled when she realized they'd worked out an understanding.

For her.

"Thank you," she whispered. "Thank you for everything."

"Sit. I'll get you something to drink, then we'll go

over what happened yesterday. Do you want coffee, juice, cocoa, water, soda?"

"Juice," she decided quickly. She made her way to the table and sat beside Zoey, and across from Vi and Mary. She looked at the small table and the crush of people within the room.

Men she hadn't met had quietly shuffled into the room at some point and were standing in the corner the women had vacated. No, that wasn't right. She'd seen Jud and Gage. But there were two more she hadn't met yet with them. Voices drifted in from the other room, which meant even more people.

Ethan set orange juice down in front of her and sat on a stool he dragged from the bar. He pushed a button on the side, and she watched in surprise as the legs shortened.

"Cool," Zoey breathed. "I want one."

"A buddy of ours designed them. We helped fund it, so we got a few as a thank you," Milo offered. "There's a bunch more in the garage we haven't assembled. Grab one if you want."

"Sweet." The woman grinned, then looked at her two counterparts across the way. "Tex called. He and Cord finished their part."

"Jacob's already fed it into HERA. We got the alert a little while ago," Vi said as she glanced at her cellphone. "We should have a better idea what happened soon enough.'

"The women and Tex hacked all the security camera feeds in South and East Austin and pulled the footage. Their system is going to run through it and gather any footage that has either Chester or Samual Rivers. We'll add other people if needed until we get some answers," Ethan explained.

The back door opened before Mari could respond. Jen entered. Two handsome men entered behind her. Ethan stood and met them halfway into the room.

"Good to see you, Dax." He shook the first man's hand and they did a man greeting, half-hug maneuver.

Mari froze when her gaze settled on the second man. Detective Rodriguez.

"Detective, I have to admit this is a surprise.'

"Mr. Davenport," he returned in greeting. His gaze settled on Mari. "Ms. Santos."

"I take it this is an official visit," Ethan said as he regarded Daxton. "Mari, this is Daxton Chambers, of the Texas Rangers."

She'd figured that much out thanks to the badge on his dark green, button-down shirt. The material accentuated his muscular frame well, as did the black slacks. His brown hair was cut short and he was about the same height as Ethan. The wedding ring glinted on his finger. She couldn't help but notice the way his thumb stroked its underside.

She smiled at him and the detective even though she wanted them gone. They'd been having a good morning and nothing they could say would add to that.

"What's wrong?" she asked, deciding to get the point rather than let the pleasantries drag out.

"Marisol!" Her mother shouted from the kitchen. "You do not treat guests like that. I raised you better. Forgive my daughter, she is shy."

The two men smiled as they headed toward the table and took the two seats Vi and Mary vacated. Ethan took Zoey's. The room suddenly shrank as she regarded the two men who had just arrived. Then she glanced at Jen and saw the tentative smile.

Okay, so maybe it wasn't all bad news.

"I'm afraid we need to ask you a few questions about your ex-husband," Detective Rodriguez said. "Does he have any properties at his disposal not in his name?"

"You're looking for him," she replied.

"Any information you have would help," Daxton offered.

"He has quite a few cousins in San Antonio. I can't remember where exactly, but their place is south of town, off Interstate 35. Cooter Rollins is the uncle's name, I believe. He owns the property as far as I know." Mari looked at Daxton, then over at Detective Rodriguez. "He has a lot of friends, but I don't know all their names I'm afraid."

"I take it he's being brought in for questioning," Ethan said.

"Yes." Daxton looked over at the corner at the women and smirked. "I'm not sure exactly what happened yesterday evening, but the Department of Defense and Homeland Security are all over the APD now. They've demanded a full investigation of the Homicide Division. And the Burglary and Robbery Divisions as well. The order apparently came straight from the top, the Secretary of Defense."

"That *Bob*," Milo laughed from the kitchen.

Daxton quirked his eyebrows, as did Mari. She looked over at Ethan, who was grinning at the women in the corner. Vi and Mary both shrugged. The men around them chuckled.

"Don't ask," Zoey supplied.

"Investigations of that magnitude take a significant amount of time," Daxton explained. "We won't have a resolution for a while, but all investigations involving you and Counterstrike have been closed due to lack of evidence."

"They had no justification to go after you or Counterstrike, Ms. Santos," Detective Rodriguez admitted. "I'm saying that off the record because you deserve to know. Last night's actions are being added to the investigation into Mr. Rollins."

Mari breathed a relieved sigh and nodded. "I wish I could do more to help find him."

"You've done more than you realize. Your statements have helped tremendously. I'm not in your official investigation," Dax said. "The two assigned to assist are the best around. They'll keep the investigation on track."

"Thank you," she offered lamely.

"Did he ever mention an ex-wife by chance?" Dax asked.

"No." Her gut soured. "He was married? Before me?"

She glanced around as the two men regarded one another. The information should've surprised her, but it didn't. Chester was a bastard who would've likely gotten off on not telling her he'd been married before. "I didn't know."

"I'm thinking this information isn't in the good column," Jud commented from the corner.

Dax shifted his attention there. "We can't discuss the details."

The man glanced down at Vi and grinned. "That's okay. We'll figure it out on our own."

"We figured as much," Detective Rodriguez commented. "You'll be contacted by the official investigators shortly, but we both wanted you to know the tide has shifted after last night's...incident. I hope you don't judge the entire APD by the actions of a few."

It was more than a few, but Mari remained silent. In all honesty, she had judged the entire department by the actions of those who'd tormented her on Chester's behalf.

"An extensive investigation into your experiences will begin shortly," Dax said. "Chester is the primary concern, but the others are just as culpable. They had a duty to protect and serve you and they failed. We'll make every effort to ensure it doesn't happen again."

"Appreciated," Ethan said.

"You've got a good man and a great group behind you now, Ms. Santos. Trust them and they'll help you get through this. We all will," Daxton said. "Perhaps when this is all over someone can explain to me how this house became a matter of national security that went as high up as the Secretary of Defense."

"You don't want to know. I keep saying that and no one listens," Zoey said. "Yeesh."

Gage chuckled. "Leave them be, Little Bit."

"For the love of all that's holy, stop calling me that."

Everyone in the corner laughed. Mari smiled. Her mother approached Daxton and Detective Rodriguez. Her fingers stroked the cross around her neck.

"What's her name?" her mom asked.

"Excuse me, ma'am?" Detective Rodriguez asked.

"The ex-wife, before my *hija*." She looked up at the man and flashed her ten-thousand-watt smile, the one that could conquer worlds if she wished. "I will pray for her. What is her name."

"I'm afraid we can't—"

"Sandra Gomez, from Devine," Daxton cut in with a grin. "I'm thinking that's enough information for God to work with."

"Bueno, he'll make do." Her mom patted Daxton's arm. "You are a good boy. *Gracias* for protecting my daughter. Sit, we will have breakfast. *Mijo*, fix coffee."

Mari froze at the term for son. She looked at her mom and noted her gaze on Ethan. Oh boy. Mom was cutting corners. She'd been after her to start dating for a while now. Clearly she'd put two and two together and jumped clear to four hundred.

"I'm afraid we must go, Mrs. Santos. Another time," Dax said as he looked at Ethan. "You need anything, let us know. Lots of folks in San Antonio are willing to make the short trip up here if needed."

"Appreciated." Ethan nodded toward the corner. "Tex has us covered."

The room settled into a tense silence as Ethan escorted the two men to the door. He latched it shut behind them and turned to regard his sister. "Well?"

"It's a step in the right direction, but it'll be a long road mired in red tape."

"At least they realize last night's move was bogus," Milo said.

"Bueno. Bueno," Mari's mom said. She pointed at the corner. "You. Sandra Gomez. Devine." Then she pointed at Milo. "Chop. *Mi hija* needs to eat."

The women looked at one another and the men all laughed as they shuffled from the corner. One of them stooped down and picked up a laptop case. He smirked as he handed it to Mary.

"I'm thinking you have your marching orders."

"Don't tease, Dylan. She's in protective mama mode," Zoey whispered. "I've seen it before. Women can do anything when their baby's cornered. Let's get to work. I'm thinking her so-called prayer was a ruse."

Oh boy.

Mari intercepted her mom halfway to the corner. She wasn't sure what she intended, but there was no way all that brawn in the corner was about to let her mom lay into the women. "Mom, let's fix breakfast. I'm hungry."

"God works in mysterious ways. You don't question his plan. You do his bidding." She shook a finger toward the corner in general. "Get to work."

Work. Mari dreaded the conversation she needed to have. She glanced at Ethan.

"No way in hell you're going to work today, Mari. Don't even think it," Jen said. "I backed that decision yesterday and look what happened. You're staying here at the house, or you're going to Counterstrike and helping us there, but you aren't working."

The woman had a point. Things did technically happen while she was at work, or started there at least. And she had to admit she was more than a little curious to see Counterstrike's headquarters. It was an important part of Ethan's life, which meant she wanted to know more.

Ethan leaned in until his hot breath fanned along the shell of her ear. A shiver of anticipation rolled through her as her mind wandered back to the amazing kissing they'd had. Her toes curled in her tennis shoes. "Whatever you decide to do today, sweetheart, you're mine tonight. We're going out on a date. A real one."

A date?

Panic filled her at the thought. She had nothing to wear on a date. She hadn't been out on one in forever. Months. No. Years. She swallowed and dutifully nodded. She'd figure it out. Surely one of her credit cards could eek out enough room for something. Right?

Zoey trundled over and patted her on the back when Ethan headed into the kitchen to make coffee. "Don't worry, girlfriend. We'll sneak out and take you shopping."

"I don't think I should sneak out anywhere. Ethan would probably send ninjas to come find me or something."

"It'll be fine. Trust me." The woman grinned big,

like she'd just planned the heist of the century and gotten away with it. Mari couldn't help but smile back. The woman's upbeat mindset was infectious. "We'll take your mom."

Shopping with mom and a new friend sounded fun, which was something else she hadn't had much of lately. "That sounds perfect."

She glanced over at Ethan in the kitchen and noted the way he and Milo watched. She didn't think Zoey was as under the radar for a planned shopping outing as she thought.

But it didn't matter because Mari had a date with Ethan tonight.

CHAPTER 10

THE WOMEN ENTERED THE MILLIONTH SHOP. SIX hours and they were still shopping. Ethan glared over at Milo as he walked into the small boutique behind them.

"There's a special place in hell for people who like shopping," Mary stated as she sat beside him on the bench.

Mary. After the first couple of hours his mind had shifted from thinking of her as Edge to seeing her as Mary. Nolan chuckled from beside him. The three had formed a ritual of sitting outside wherever the women landed. Jen, Zoey, Mari, and her mom were having a blast shopping. Vi flitted between their group and Mary's.

Dylan and the other men had trusted Nolan, Ethan, and Milo to keep them safe while they went through and double-checked installation on all the security cameras in the empty safehouses. Jud had joined them at the last minute.

"Thank you," he said. "For what you're doing for Counterstrike. For Mari. For what you did to get me out of that jungle. Thank you."

"We should have some answers when we get back to the house—assuming the shopping doesn't kill us," Mary said. "Tex and Jacob are close to getting what we need. HERA's pulled all the footage we needed. Now it's just a matter of putting the pieces together."

"It's a hell of a system."

"It's due for upgrades. That's on the agenda over the next few months, once things settle down at The Arsenal."

"Like that'll ever happen," Nolan muttered.

Mary chuckled. "Trouble does have a way of finding us."

"More like we have a way of knocking it over, kneeing it in the nuts, and kicking its ass," Jud said as he sat on the ground beside the bench. "The women are checking out. Mari walked in and fell in love with a dress immediately. Thank fuck."

Ethan smiled as he looked at the small boutique. He couldn't wait to take Mari out tonight, to get her mind on something other than her bastard ex and the other shit swirling around them all.

That kiss.

His entire body tightened whenever he thought about it. Blood surged southward of its own accord. The woman was breathtaking. He'd been with more women than he cared to remember. None had ever made him react so quickly and easily.

"I hope to hell taking her out tonight isn't a mistake. They haven't found the bastard yet," Ethan said. "Twitch and Milo said they'd keep an eye on us, just in case."

"You'll be covered. I'm thinking Vi needs a night on the town," Jud commented.

"I could go for a steak. Baby needs a thick slab of something bloody," Mary commented.

"At least you aren't puking your guts out every few minutes," Jud commented.

Ethan wondered what Mari would be like pregnant. She'd be a great mom. Jesus, he was in deep. He was already imagining the two of them together years from now. Married.

With kids.

It was way too soon for those sort of thoughts, but he was naturally impulsive. No, decisive.

"Love happens when we least expect it," Mary commented. "It's something I've learned lately."

"No shit," Jud said. "Some free advice, just go with it. Surrendering is easier. You can't fight fate."

SEVEN HOURS LATER

ETHAN WASN'T SURE WHETHER TO KICK THE WOMEN'S asses or kiss them all for helping Mari get ready. She sauntered down the stairwell looking like a queen adorned in a jade green dress that hugged her generous curves. Blood surged to his cock.

Her long, curly hair spiraled around her face in softer, looser twirls that ended with a flirt across her breasts. If he looked hard enough he could see the bruising and marks left by the bastard who'd hurt her, but someone had done a hell of a job concealing them with makeup.

Makeup. That's what was different about Mari's face. Pale pink lipstick accentuated her thick, lush lips. Her eyes seemed bigger, brighter. She offered a hesitant smile as she descended the last step. He reached out and took her hand.

"You're gorgeous, sweetheart." He leaned in and feathered a kiss across her forehead.

He wanted to toss her over his shoulder and cart her to his bedroom caveman style, but he didn't think the group of people clustered around them would be down with that decision. Someone cleared their throat behind him. He glanced over his shoulder and took the thin, lacy shawl his sister offered.

In the hour the women took helping her get ready, he'd worked out a protection detail with everyone else. Mary, Dylan, Jud and Vi would follow in Milo's car. Getting reservations for three separate tables for the same time last minute at the trendy lakeside restaurant he'd planned had proven almost impossible.

Fortunately the Davenport name still carried more weight than Ethan cared to admit. Or use. Either way, reservations had been secured. Zoey, Gage, Twitch and Jet were secondary support. Ethan still wasn't sure how Zoey had finagled her way into the mix, but he was assured by all The Arsenal folks she'd prove useful with the surveillance drones.

Drones they'd handed over to them just a few

hours ago as a "just in case they are ever needed." Ethan was a bit overwhelmed by their generosity and trust. Milo had admitted earlier he broke into hives thinking about keeping all the high-security-clearance equipment they'd been given secure. If anyone ever caught wind of the fact they had it...

Ethan pushed the thought back and wrapped the shawl around Mari. "You ready?"

"I think so."

"Here's your clutch. There's a tracker chip in there, and on your earrings. And there's one on Ethan's lapel and his keyring," Mary said. "It was Tex's idea, just in case. The signals are synced to HERA and Tex's system, so you're double-covered."

"So beautiful," her mom whispered. She patted Mari's unbruised cheek softly as she kissed her other side. "Have fun. Dance for me."

Ethan had to admit he enjoyed the idea of holding her close, moving with her in rhythm to music. He put an arm at her waist and willed his desire to manageable levels. At this rate the date would be the shortest in history, just so he could get her alone. Not that that would happen anytime soon since they had a houseful of people.

"The coms have a five-mile radius on them, so

don't worry if you don't see us," Vi offered. "We'll be close enough, but far enough away."

Thank God.

Ethan flashed a grateful smile at the group and escorted Mari out to his car. His heartbeat accelerated as a burst of adrenaline shot through his system. He'd fought wars and been less nervous. He'd spent less time planning battles than he had a simple dinner with Mari.

But nothing with Mari would ever be simple because she deserved the best. For the first time in a long while he was grateful he was in a position to give her precisely that.

MARI HAD NEVER LAUGHED SO MUCH. HER SIDES AND face ached from the merriment, but she wouldn't trade the pain for anything in the world. Wild Basin was a trendy restaurant focused on meats of all kinds. She was a bit surprised by his choice of restaurants until he pointed at Mary and whispered, "The baby likes meat."

Another huge part of her fell in love with him instantly hearing his reply. He'd chosen the restaurant because a woman he barely knew, one who'd gone out of her way to help Mari, was pregnant and craving meat.

The date progressed from there. The courses arrived one after another after another after another. The endless supply of tasty food was only surpassed by the easy conversation and delightful man she was with. He was brilliant, passionate, engaging, patient, understanding, and so many other things.

Including curious. He asked her endless questions about everything and anything. No topic was off the table, including politics. They'd debated current events. He'd listened to her side and presented his own, which wasn't much different than hers.

He valued her opinion.

He listened.

Because she mattered.

And they danced.

The restaurant clearly wasn't intended for dancing, but it didn't matter. He'd stood, winked, and pulled her to him. And they waltzed.

When patrons started looking, Dylan and Mary joined in, then Vi and Jud. The entire experience was overwhelmingly perfect.

She looked across the small table nestled in the

corner of the restaurant and smiled. "Ethan, I can't eat another bite."

"Just one. I swear this is the best dessert ever created," he said as he forked a piece of the decadent mousse he'd ordered and held it out.

Mari leaned forward and wrapped her mouth around the small spoon. A moan escaped her as the tastes and sensations exploded within her mouth. Her eyes widened as she looked down at the small dish. She'd never tasted anything so delicious.

He chuckled. "The chef who makes them has been offered countless opportunities in L.A., New York, Paris, and anywhere else he could imagine. But he remains here in Austin because of his family."

"This is amazing," she whispered. "I'll never think of dessert the same. Nothing will ever compare to this."

"We'll come here whenever you want," he promised.

Just like that, he'd affirmed once again his desire to continue seeing her. He'd dropped statements like that into the conversation many times throughout the evening, as if assuring her whatever she might be feeling was mutual.

While she was relieved in many ways, she was also concerned. She wasn't a high-society socialite.

Although she didn't pretend to understand every-thing inherent with having the last name Davenport, she'd seen enough tonight to know it was a big deal.

Until they'd arrived at the restaurant he'd been Ethan, the amazing man who'd waded into her trou-bles and guided her to firm ground. Her protector.

But everyone treated him like royalty at the restaurant. The manager, head chef, and almost every patron had made their way to the small table for one reason or another. He handled each intru-sion with grace and patience.

"How is your mousse, Mr. Davenport?" The manager's voice punctured Mari's dreamlike state once again.

"Fine," Ethan clipped with less patience than the last three times the man had come over. "Thank you. I believe we have everything we need."

"Of course." The man hovered despite the obvious dismissal. Mari blotted her mouth with her linen napkin, then reached over and took Ethan's hand.

He squeezed hers in return as his jaw twitched.

"Did you need something?" Ethan asked.

"We have a charity event this next weekend, for the children's hospital. I have a video recorder in the back. If you could spare a few moments to offer a few kind words about our upcoming event, it'd help so much, Mr. Davenport. I hate to trouble you, but it's for the children." The man hesitated. "Your father was always a staunch supporter."

"Of course he was," Ethan countered, agitation in his voice. "I'll be there in a minute."

"Of course. Thank you, sir. No doubt you've saved lives tonight with your gracious acceptance." The man shuffled away.

Talk about weird. Mari ran her hand along Ethan's arm. "Are you okay?"

"Honestly?"

"I wouldn't want you to lie," she countered with a smile. "Talk to me."

"I hate the societal games I'm forced to play because of my last name. Milo and I bankrupted the bastard, one business at a time. We crumbled his empire, but nothing we did could touch his name. That will continue to live on, because it's too steeped in society."

"Then change it for the better."

Ethan sighed and cupped her face. "You have no idea what a treasure you are, Mari. You are right. That's the only thing we can do at this point, which is why I hate moments like this. All I wanted was to take you out for dinner and give you a beautiful night."

"You have," she whispered. "The best I've ever had."

"Even with all the interruptions?"

She shrugged. "I just pretended I was sitting with Christian Grey."

Ethan grinned wickedly. "Oh, really?"

"We'll discuss my Christian Grey thoughts after you go in and do your good deed for the evening," she teased, a bit surprised she could be so brazen with a man.

No. With Ethan.

She had a feeling she could do anything with him. She smiled as he headed toward the back, following the strange manager flitting about near the entrance to the kitchen area. She took a sip of her wine and listened as Ethan tried to calm the agitated man down.

"I had no choice, Mr. Davenport. I'm sorry."

"No heroics or she eats a bullet." Mari froze as Chester's voice came over the com.

"Please. He'll kill me. He's already killed Manuel." The woman's terrified voice kicked Mari's pulse into triple step.

"Let's go," Dylan said, suddenly appearing at her table.

She peered up at him like he'd grown two heads and morphed into a dragon. "I'm not leaving. He has Ethan."

"That's exactly why you're leaving. We'll handle Chester, assuming Ethan doesn't do it himself when given an opening. The plan in case something went sideways was clear. You're evacuated and secured."

"I never agreed to that," she argued, standing to her full five foot four (thanks to the two-inch heels). "Find another plan because I'm not going anywhere."

"This isn't smart, Chester. You aren't getting Mari," Ethan said in the com.

"I don't want that fat cunt, not anymore. I came here to teach her one last lesson, one I thought would end with a bullet between your eyes. But I'm starting to see there's a better, much more profitable exit strategy for me, isn't there?"

"You want money to run," Ethan said. "Fair enough. Tell me what you want and I'll make it happen. But you've got to let everyone back here go first. Be smart, man. You can't keep ten hostages secured, especially when one of them is former Delta."

"Shut up!" Chester shouted. "You're just like her! Always knowing better than me. Always saying what I should do!"

"Fine, you want to keep ten people at gun point with a stupid little .45, go for it. You'll probably want to move away from that exit though. Or move us. This place is a nightmare. There's a window between two rear exits, not to mention the two into the dining area. Ten hostages, five potential egresses and one .45. Jesus, you are as dumb as she said you were."

A boom echoed through the mic.

Dylan cursed, snagged her arm, and dragged her toward the restaurant's exit as the rest of the patrons panicked. He looked at Mary. "Get her outside. Vi, you go with them. Jud, you're with me. This shit ends now."

"I'm not going anywhere. Let me go." Mari kicked and screamed and turned to face where Ethan had gone. "Chester, you worthless son of a bitch, come out and face me like a man once and for all. Stop cowering behind your cronies."

Mari heard the cursing and grunting through the com. Terror clawed up her throat and made breathing impossible. What was happening?

"Stupid fucking cunt! Never learns. Gotta teach her a lesson. Get up, you stupid fucking bastard. Up!

Now!" Rustling sounded through the com. "Not such a hotshot shit after all, huh? Fucking Deltas. Always think you're better than everyone. I showed you. You'll be dead in five minutes, but I want the bitch to see your last breath and know it's her fault. She's mine. You shouldn't have gotten between me and her."

Mari gasped when the kitchen doors swung open and a wild-eyed Chester exited with Ethan stretched across his front. Ethan's glare swept across the room, but Mari's gaze settled on the spurting blood from his leg.

Oh no. No. No. No.

"Fuck," Jud spat angrily. "We've got about a minute before he bleeds out. Angle's wrong for us to take a shot from this distance."

"Stand down," Dylan ordered, gun drawn.

Mari was on the move, charging toward Ethan and Chester. Chester's focus shifted toward her.

"Stay back, bitch. This is because of you! All you had to do was obey me. Accept you were mine," Chester shouted.

"Let him go," she pleaded. "Please, let him go."

A shadow shifted along the floor. Mari didn't bother trying to figure out who or what it was. She just prayed they were there to save Ethan. Tears streamed down her face as she forced herself to her knees like Chester always liked.

"Please, Chester. Please. I'm begging you. Let him go."

"Now that's better, cunt. But too late. You've gotta learn."

A gunshot exploded. She screamed out as she tried to make sense of what she'd missed in the microsecond she'd been looking at the floor. Blood coated her skin, her face. Her eyes. She blinked and stared at the two bodies on the floor across from her.

She crawled, ignoring the blood covering her.

Ethan.

Have to get to Ethan.

Twitch crouched down and flipped Ethan over. His dark brown eyes settled on Mari a moment as he undid Ethan's tie. "Get his belt."

Belt. Right.

She didn't ask why. The why didn't matter. If Twitch wanted a belt, she'd dang sure get one. Her mind was numb. Her entire body was numb as shock settled in and her fight or flight response kicked into overdrive.

She yanked the belt off, then noted the blood still spurting from Ethan's leg. God. No. No. No. She wrestled to get it around his leg as Twitch hoisted him up enough for the leather to wrap around.

Twitch threaded the tie through a loop on each end, then looked down into Ethan's eyes just as he opened them. "Sorry, man, this is gonna hurt."

"Ethan." Mari touched his face with her bloody hand. "You're going to be okay."

His scream tore through her as Twitch yanked the makeshift tourniquet closed. Mari silently thanked whatever fate made Ethan pass out. She ran a hand across his forehead and watched as Dylan, Jud and Twitch worked on him. The latter had a small container of something which looked a lot like crazy glue, but surely it wasn't.

She tried to stay out of the way as best as she could, but not being there wasn't an option. She needed to touch him, affirm the fact he was alive. Her fingers grazed his wrist until she found a pulse. Slow. Slower.

God.

"Mari, come on, sweetheart. We need to get you outside. The ambulance is on the way," Vi said.

"No, I'm not leaving him." She shook her head and dared anyone to be stupid enough to try and make her leave.

Tears streamed down her face as her focus

tunneled on the weakening pulse beneath her fingertips. This was her fault. No.

She looked over at Chester's dead body. The bastard was finally dead.

She only hoped it wasn't too late for Ethan.

CHAPTER 11

THE PRESTIGIOUS, PRIVATE HOSPITAL NEAR THE LAKE was nothing like South Austin Emergency. The Chief Surgeon had greeted Ethan and the emergency personnel at the double entry doors to the emergency area. They'd whisked Ethan away and made Mari wait on the other side of a second set of double doors.

That was three hours ago.

She paced.

Milo, Twitch, Zoey, Vi, and Mary had all tried to drag her into conversation. Make her sit. Make her eat something.

The excuse was always different, but the objective was the same—keep her attention away from the fact they hadn't heard anything about Ethan.

"Hija."

Crap. Mari squeezed her eyes shut as her mom drew her into a hug. She was still covered in blood and hadn't given a damn about that fact. But she didn't want her mom witnessing all this. The aftermath of the final battle.

Chester was dead.

She was too terrified about Ethan's prognosis for that fact to settle in.

"Come, we'll get you showered and changed."

Mari shook her head. "No. They'll come out soon. I want to be here."

"We'll come get you the second they come out," Zoey promised. "You don't want him waking up and seeing you like this, sweetie. No man should see his woman bathed in blood, especially if most of it is his. Trust me, I know a thing or two about this."

"She's right," Chatter offered as he stopped beside Zoey. "There's a shower right down the hall the nurses said you could use. Ethan's tough. He's not going anywhere. The sooner you clean up, the faster you'll find out how he's doing."

It was the most words the man had ever uttered in her presence.

"You promise?" Mari looked around the small waiting area they'd been taken to.

"We promise," Jen said. "Go. My brother's too stubborn to die."

"Come," her mom ordered. "Zoey and I will help."

She'd been showering herself since she was a kid, but she obediently trundled down the hall in her bare feet and let her mom and Zoey steer her wherever the mythical shower was. Mari didn't remember taking her shoes off.

She didn't remember much, to be perfectly honest.

Shock.

Chester was dead.

She continued to bookend the evening with that thought every now and then to remind herself her ordeal was over. She hoped.

As long as Ethan was okay, she'd be okay.

The realization seeped down deep, settled in her heart and grew. They'd known each other for such a short amount of time, but she wanted to explore their attraction. She wanted to be a part of Ethan's world.

Because he mattered to her.

Because she mattered to him.

Mari didn't realize how out of it she was until her mom and Zoey shoved her into the shower. They'd managed to get her dress and undergarments off without her even noticing.

They must have trusted she was alert enough to handle washing herself thanks to the pelting of warm water against her skin. She let the tears she'd held back flow as the heat from the shower sloughed off enough of her shock for reality to return. For her fears to collide with the fact she didn't want to speculate the worst-case scenario.

She's survived for years by planning strategies based on assuming the worst case. But her brain refused to plan the worst-case scenario today.

Because that meant Ethan was dead.

She scrubbed and soaped until the water going down the drain was clear. She toweled dry and stepped into the scrubs left on the small counter nearest the shower. Clean, she exited the bathroom.

Chatter was heading toward them down the hall. Her feet moved double-time toward him.

"The surgeon just came out to talk to us. Jen made him wait until we got you," he said.

Jen made him wait. Mari's heart swelled. She wasn't family. Jen and Milo could've easily let him give them an update, even if they'd promised otherwise.

But good people didn't lie. They abided by their promises because they gave a damn about the person they'd made them to. Mari let that fact sink in.

She mattered to Ethan, but she also mattered to Jen, Milo and the others.

Because she mattered to Ethan.

Somehow the echoing thought in her brain helped keep her calm as she shuffled down the hall as fast as the too-long pants allowed.

Milo was closest to her in the huddle and she took in his presence like a punch to the gut. God, he did look so much like Ethan, more so tonight. He'd lost the glint in his gaze. He squatted down before her and she stood frozen as he rolled up the pants legs of her scrubs.

He stood and smirked. "Can't have you falling. Ethan would kick my ass."

Mari hoped to hell Ethan would be up to doing precisely that soon. She looked expectantly at the surgeon standing before the larger-than-Mari-realized crowd of waiting people.

"The surgery was touch and go, but Ethan made it through. He lost a large amount of blood, but the field work saved his life. Recovery will be slow, but he's through the worst of it." The man looked around. "He's still awaking from surgery, but he's quite vocal. Is there a Mari here?"

She gulped. Tears filled her eyes. Ethan was going to be okay. The cluster of people parted and slowly guided her closer to the surgeon.

"Ah, yes. You must be Mari. Come with me. He's demanded to see you, assuming he's still awake. We expected him to sleep for another few hours before he was fully alert and ready for visitors, but he's quite determined to see you."

That sounded exactly like Ethan—more worried about her than himself. She reached for Jen. "Can she and his brother come with me? Please?"

"This is highly irregular," the surgeon responded.

Milo cleared his throat and pointed a finger at the wall. Mari thought the gesture was odd, then she saw the plaque on the wall. The Davenport Wing.

They'd funded this wing of the hospital?

The motion activated the surgeon. He nodded and the newly formed group of her, Jen, and Milo headed down a long, white corridor that stunk of antiseptic and...hospital. She didn't know how else to describe it.

If she ever had a bajillion dollars she'd figure out

a way to make hospitals smell like roses. Or begonias. Anything but this. She muttered the thought as she followed the fast-walking doctor.

Milo's laughter boomed within the narrow corridor. "I'll see what we can do about that."

The momentary bit of humor helped slough off the worst of her fear. Ethan was going to be okay. Chester was dead.

It was over.

Now they could move on with their lives, whatever that translated to. With all luck, she could continue getting to know Ethan. The doctor halted at the end of the long corridor and motioned toward the room on the left.

Mari's heart leapt into her throat as her pulse quickened. Tears streaming down her face, she turned the corner and vaulted into the room. Relief assailed her as she forced a ragged breath and studied the sleeping man on the bed.

"His body's been through quite an ordeal. It'll likely be a while before he wakes again," the doctor said in a whisper. "I can let you know when he wakes up."

"No." Mari quietly moved a chair as close to the bed as she could and sat. "I'll wait."

"Ma'am, I'm afraid you need to return to the waiting area," he said.

"She'll wait here. We will all wait here. Thank you," Jen said, her tone dismissive. "Please have someone bring in another couple of seats and one of the sleeper recliners. Oh, and a meal of some sort. She'll need to eat in a few minutes."

"Yes, ma'am, of course."

Mari was grateful Jen had handled the doctor. Eyes watery, she breathed another deep breath and grasped Ethan's hand. It was limp, but warm. She threaded their fingers through one another and reached over with her other hand until her finger grazed the pulse point along his wrist.

Eyes closed, she began the slow glide. One letter at a time.

ETHAN BLINKED AWAKE. HE WAS HIGHER THAN HELL. He recognized the feeling from the injuries he'd sustained while fleeing the jungle prison. Aw hell.

He knifed up out of bed and froze as his vision settled on Mari. Thank fuck. He collapsed back on the bed.

"She hasn't left your side," Milo whispered. He

made his way to the side of the bed. "We took turns staying in here with her, but she hasn't left. She passed out a couple hours ago. You were out a while. You got an infection."

"How long?" His throat hurt like hell. He swallowed as he ran his fingers through her hair.

"Two days. You've been in and out of it, mostly out. You went through a patch where you thought you'd just gotten back from the jungle. You made a hell of a mess."

"You didn't tell them I reacted badly to painkillers," he said.

"I did, but they felt it was worth the risk. We all agreed." Milo smirked. "Nolan and I got you back down. You responded to him, probably because he was there back then."

Shit.

"She's damn near written an entire book on your wrist," Milo commented. "You're skin'll likely be sore. Then again, maybe not. She's used almost a whole bottle of lotion on you."

He reached down and ran his hands through her hair and grasped firmly enough to draw her attention. She needed her sleep, but he needed her to know he was okay more.

Mari's head popped off the bed. Beautiful brown eyes widened and latched onto him.

"Ethan." She breathed his name and cupped his face. "You're awake. Finally."

"I'm okay, sweetheart. I'm sorry I scared you. You should be at home resting."

She shook her head. "I wasn't leaving until you woke up. I have it on good authority that seeing a friendly face when you're waking up somewhere strange is always welcome, especially after you've had a scare."

Ethan reeled as he took in her smile. He processed her statement, remembered when he'd said it to her back when everything started and he'd had Twitch bring June Bug.

She remembered.

Word for fucking word, she remembered.

"I'm sorry you got shot," she whispered. "You're going to be okay, though. Jen and I found the best physical therapist around. The bullet did quite a bit of damage, but it's nothing you can't fully recover from. We have a plan. Or, well, several."

He smiled. It sounded like little sis had worked hard to keep Mari's mind focused on the future rather than watching him rot away in a hospital bed.

"Status?"

"Chester's dead. Investigation's ongoing. So far they've suspended three detectives in Homicide and two in Robbery. The blue's rolling over on them. No one wants the foul taste of what he did stinking up the APD," Milo said.

"Jen's worked out a settlement with the police department for me. I told her I didn't want anything from them, but she said I should take it." Mari squeezed his hand. "So I did. She's going to help me start a nonprofit to run in conjunction with Counterstrike. I want to educate and train the women you're helping, so they can get better jobs."

Ethan smiled. "That's a wonderful idea, sweetheart."

And a pricey one. Either Jen had negotiated one hell of a settlement with the APD on Mari's behalf, or little sis and big-bro-by-two-minutes had quietly added a couple zeroes to get her dream started.

"I'll go let the others know you're awake and alert for real this time," Milo said as he shuffled from the room.

Ethan squeezed Mari's arm. "Come up on the bed with me, sweetheart. I need to hold you in my arms."

"Okay, but let me lock the door. Last time I crawled into your bed, Nurse Cratchet got mad at me." Ethan chuckled as Mari quickly locked the door and then crawled into the bed on his "good side."

Fuck. Physical therapy was gonna suck, but he'd endure it for her.

He'd do just about anything for her.

"I was so worried, Ethan," she whispered against his neck as she settled against him. Hand around his chest, she peered up into his gaze. "I know it's too soon, and I don't know how, but I've fallen in love with you, Ethan Evans Davenport."

"I love you, too, Marisol Santos," he whispered. He claimed her mouth in a kiss too passionate for the scant amount of time they had alone.

He doubted Jen and the team would wait long to enter and see for themselves he was okay. The road to recovery would be a long, pain in the ass, but well worth it.

"The second I'm out of here, we're going out on another first date."

She smiled. "You promise?"

"This time we'll do something quiet, out of the way. No pretention. No security risks. No gunshots."

"As long as it ends with me in your bed, we can do McDonald's for all I care," she whispered.

Ethan threw his head back and laughed. Mari was hysterical because he knew she meant every word. She didn't give a damn what they did as long as they were together.

"God, I love you, sweetheart."

CHAPTER 12

THREE WEEKS LATER

MARI FRITZED AND FUSSED WITH HER HAIR, THEN pulled on the snug red dress. Tonight was finally the night. After three long weeks she was finally going out on another first date with Ethan.

Recovery had been slow and far more painful than she'd expected. Physical therapy was a special level of hell she wouldn't wish on anyone—except maybe Chester. Ethan took whatever the therapist threw at him.

She'd learned more than she ever wanted about the type of injury Ethan barely avoided sustaining.

Unbeknownst to her, a millimeter or two more to the side and he would've bled out.

She forced the thought aside.

All that mattered now was that he was alive and okay. He and Jen had switched houses. Jen was now on the second floor of the three-story house he and Milo owned, while he'd taken over the bungalow next door.

For now.

Ethan made his dislike for the arrangement quite clear. Then Mari had pointed out that it'd give them more privacy. Privacy they'd both enjoyed very, very much.

But they hadn't had sex yet.

Ethan was adamant he wasn't going to rush them, which Mari loved him for. But if they didn't make love tonight? Well, a woman had needs and he was going to find out exactly what happened when they didn't get met.

She smiled at the soft knock on the bedroom door. She'd moved into the bungalow's second bedroom. At first, sharing a house with a man she loved but wasn't sleeping with was a bit...awkward. But after a couple days they'd fallen into a comfortable routine. They spent their evenings together watching television while they mostly made out.

CARA CARNES

Her hand trembled as she turned the knob and opened the door. "Hi."

Ethan's eyes widened as his gaze drank in her new dress. She spun around so he'd get the full effect of the plunging not-there-at-all back. She'd bought it while in San Antonio, where she'd met with Zoey and a woman named Ellie. They'd had lunch and shopped their wallets dry.

It'd been worth every penny.

She memorized the hungry look in his eyes and licked her lips. "I know we're supposed to go to dinner, but there's only one thing I want tonight."

A growl rumbled from him as he grasped her head and claimed her mouth. She moaned, sagged into him, and deepened the kiss. She chased, taunted, and toyed with his tongue as she slowly drew them backward toward the bed.

She wanted him off his leg, which still bothered him late at night. The therapist had told her it'd likely be months before the pain truly went away, especially since he'd sworn off any painkillers.

Pleasure ignited along her skin as they tumbled onto the bed. She inhaled his intoxicating scent and grasped the pale gray shirt he'd put on. Feeling only a moment's guilt, she ripped it open. Buttons popped and spewed everywhere.

192

He chuckled against their connected mouths and grinned. Eyes opened, she peered into his. The slow touches he'd used earlier became demanding. Fast. Exactly what she needed.

She wanted to taste, memorize, and savor every inch of him.

"God, you're killing me," he groaned against her throat. "This dress."

The straps slid down her arms. Deft fingers unzipped the back. She leaned backward enough for the material to slide down her front.

"You're beautiful." He breathed the words as he ran kisses down her throat and across her shoulders. He cupped her breasts, breasts she'd kept hidden from him so the bitemarks could heal. She didn't want what they shared intimately tainted by the man who'd hurt her.

His thumbs raked along her nipples, flicking back and forth in a slow, sensuous glide until the achy nubs hardened. She thrust her chest forward, deepening the contact she'd imagined and fantasized about all day.

He drew one into his mouth. Pleasure arrowed downward and settled between her legs. She tasted, touched, massaged, and stroked him wherever she could.

Ethan severed contact long enough to strip out of his clothes. Magnificent. She memorized every ridge, every flex and bulge of muscle along his powerful body. Her gaze skittered past his injured leg. She didn't want a reminder of how close she'd come to losing him. Not tonight.

Tonight was a celebration of life.

Love.

"You keep looking at me like that and this will be a much shorter union than I want it to be," he mumbled with a grin.

"Nothing about you is short." She skimmed the dress past her hips and tossed it to the side of the bed. "I've waited long enough, Ethan. I need you."

"Not any more than I need you, sweetheart."

She kissed him hungrily and ran her hand down his bare chest. She wrapped her fingers around his hard, long length.

"You're a little minx," he whispered as he dragged her legs up until she fell on her back. He pinned her hands over her head and grinned. "I get to play first."

Oh God.

She writhed beneath him as he caressed down her sides, along her breasts, and up her legs. His mouth followed the same trajectory, tasting, licking, and nibbling until his hot breath trailed up her inner thighs.

Mari had spent many lonely nights the past few weeks imagining his mouth on her. She'd never come close. Deft fingers spread her folds apart as he licked and teased her sensitive flesh. His tongue flicked along her clit, back and forth until her entire body quaked with the need to come.

As if sensing her hesitation, he sped up the pace, then switched to a gentle sucking that spiraled her over the edge. Her entire body shook with her release. Fingers in his short hair, she hung on and rode the waves of pleasure.

"Ethan." She whispered his name as she cried out.

His mouth claimed hers. The carnal taste of herself on his lips made her groan. She reached between them and grasped his hard cock.

"Next time I play with you," she growled against his mouth. "I need you in me, Ethan. Please."

"Mari, I love you so much," he whispered. He looked down at the pile of clothes. "I need to get a condom, sweetheart."

"No." She shook her head. "I'm protected. I take a

shot. I have for years. I haven't been with anyone since I left him."

"Jesus, sweetheart. You kill me with how much you trust me to take care of you. I was tested recently and haven't been with anyone in months. I've never been with anyone without a condom."

Mari bristled and looked away. "I'm sorry. I shouldn't have…"

"Look at me, Mari," he ordered, his voice gentle. Fingers beneath her chin, he waited for her to turn her gaze back to him. "I love you more than anything. Of course I want to make love to you without anything between us, but I want you to know you are safe with me. Always. I would never, ever do anything to violate the trust you've given me. Okay?"

"I love you, Ethan. Please. Make love to me."

She kissed him. Eyes open, she watched his expression as he slid into her. A moan escaped her as he filled her fuller than she'd ever experienced. He groaned and rose to position his hands on either side of her head.

She grasped his shoulders, wrapped her legs around him and matched his powerful thrusts into her. Each one cast a brushfire of awareness through her entire body. He kissed her mouth, nibbled down her throat and along her earlobe. Teased her breasts.

She sank her fingernails into his back as she fought the need to orgasm again. She wanted to hold out, wait until he was ready.

"Fuck, I love how beautiful you look when you come. Give it to me, sweetheart."

She cried out and held onto him as a whirlwind of desire pulsated through her. She drifted within his embrace as he cried out with his own release.

Then collapsed on the bed, sated and sweaty.

Spectacular.

The word formed in her brain, followed by a thousand more to describe her feelings for Ethan and what they'd just done, but none formed on her tongue.

He kissed her cheek and drew her into his arms. "That was the best dinner I've ever had."

She smiled as she remembered his mouth on her, tasting her. She'd get a taste of him soon enough. Head on his chest, she sighed her contentment.

"Hate to say this, but we'd best get up and get some food in you. We've got to be at the airport early in the morning," he commented.

Excitement bubbled within her. Tex had tried

hard to get Joseph home weeks ago, but his team had been deep within a mission. They were finally home and taking a well-deserved leave.

Joseph was coming home.

She wasn't sure how long of a leave he was getting, or how much of it he'd spend in Austin, but she'd enjoy every single second of the time she got to spend with him. Her mom and dad had just left a couple days ago.

June Bug hopped up on the bed and curled onto the bed above her head and next to Ethan's. Mari couldn't help but chuckle as the cat's tail flicked back and forth on Ethan's face.

"I think someone's jealous of me," he commented.

"Likely so," she replied. "June Bug doesn't share easily."

"She'll deal."

Chompers jumped up on the best, did several spins and collapsed with a huff. Muzzle on paws, he looked at Mari like he'd eat her if given half a chance. "She's not the only jealous one."

"He'll deal," Ethan commented. "I love you, Mari Davenport."

Her insides clenched. She darted her gaze up at him.

"Marry me," he whispered. "While your brother is here. I don't want to waste another second of our life together, Marisol. I'll fly your parents back immediately. Whatever you want for a wedding, I'll make it happen. Say yes."

"All I want is you," she replied. "Yes. Yes. Yes."

~THE END~

Born in small-town Texas, Cara Carnes was a princess, a pirate, fashion model, actress, rock star and Jon Bon Jovi's wife all before the age of 13.

In reality, her fascination for enthralling worlds took seed somewhere amidst a somewhat dull day job and a wonderful life filled with family and friends. When she's not cemented to her chair, Cara loves travelling, photography and reading.

Newsletter|Facebook|Twitter

Sue Coletta: Hacked

KaLyn Cooper: Rescuing Melina

Liz Crowe: Marking Mariah

Jordan Dane: Redemption for Avery

Jordan Dane: Fiona's Salvation

Riley Edwards: Protecting Olivia

Riley Edwards: Redeeming Violet

Riley Edwards, Recovering Ivy

Nicole Flockton: Protecting Maria

Nicole Flockton: Guarding Erin

Nicole Flockton: Guarding Suzie

Nicole Flockton: Guarding Brielle

Casey Hagen: Shielding Nebraska

Casey Hagen: Shielding Harlow

Casey Hagen: Shielding Josie

Desiree Holt: Protecting Maddie

Kathy Ivan: Saving Sarah

Kathy Ivan: Saving Savannah

Kathy Ivan: Saving Stephanie

Jesse Jacobson: Protecting Honor

Jesse Jacobson: Fighting for Honor

Jesse Jacobson: Defending Honor

Jesse Jacobson: Summer Breeze

Silver James: Rescue Moon

Silver James: SEAL Moon

Silver James: Assassin's Moon

LeTeisha Newton: Protecting Heartbeat

MJ Nightingale: Protecting Beauty

MJ Nightingale: Betting on Benny

MJ Nightingale: Protecting Secrets

Sarah O'Rourke: Saving Liberty

Debra Parmley: Protecting Pippa

Lainey Reese: Protecting New York

Jenika Snow: Protecting Lily

Jen Talty: Burning Desire

Jen Talty: Burning Kiss

Jen Talty: Burning Skies

Jen Talty: Burning Lies

Jen Talty: Burning Heart

Megan Vernon: Protecting Us

Megan Vernon: Protecting Earth

Fire and Police: Operation Alpha World

KaLyn Cooper: Justice for Gwen

As you know, this book included at least one character from Susan Stoker's books. To check out more, see below.

Delta Force Heroes Series

Rescuing Rayne (FREE!)

Rescuing Aimee (novella)

Rescuing Emily

Rescuing Harley

Marrying Emily

Rescuing Kassie

Rescuing Bryn

Rescuing Casey

Rescuing Sadie

Rescuing Wendy

Rescuing Mary (Oct 2018)

Rescuing Macie (April 2019)

Badge of Honor: Texas Heroes Series

Justice for Mackenzie (FREE!)

Justice for Mickie

Justice for Corrie

Justice for Laine (novella)

Shelter for Elizabeth

Justice for Boone

Shelter for Adeline

Shelter for Sophie

Justice for Erin

Justice for Milena

Shelter for Blythe

Justice for Hope (Sept 2018)

Shelter for Quinn (Feb 2019)

Shelter for Koren (June 2019)

Shelter for Penelope (Oct 2019)

SEAL of Protection Series

Protecting Caroline (FREE!)

Protecting Alabama

Protecting Fiona

Marrying Caroline (novella)

Protecting Summer

Protecting Cheyenne

Protecting Jessyka

Protecting Julie (novella)

Protecting Melody

Protecting the Future

Protecting Kiera (novella)

Protecting Dakota

SEAL of Protection: Legacy Series

Securing Caite (Jan 2019)

Securing Sidney (May 2019)
Securing Piper (Sept 2019)
Securing Zoey (TBA)
Securing Avery (TBA)
Securing Kalee (TBA)

New York Times, USA Today and *Wall Street Journal* Bestselling Author Susan Stoker has a heart as big as the state of Texas where she lives, but this all American girl has also spent the last fourteen years living in Missouri, California, Colorado, and Indiana. She's married to a retired Army man who now gets to follow *her* around the country.

She debuted her first series in 2014 and quickly followed that up with the SEAL of Protection Series, which solidified her love of writing and creating stories readers can get lost in.

If you enjoyed this book, or any book, please consider leaving a review. It's appreciated by authors more than you'll know.

www.stokeraces.com
www.AcesPress.com
susan@stokeraces.com

Made in the USA
Columbia, SC
18 November 2020

24861435R00120